STAR TREK 28:
THE CRY OF THE ONLIES

D1149966

STAR TREK NOVELS

1: CHAIN OF ATTACK
2: DEEP DOMAIN
3: DREAMS OF THE RAVEN
4: THE ROMULAN WAY
5: HOW MUCH FOR JUST THE PLANET?
6: BLOODTHIRST
7: THE I.D.I.C. EPIDEMIC
8: YESTERDAY'S SON
9: TIME FOR YESTERDAY
10: THE FINAL REFLECTION
11: TIMETRAP
12: THE VULCAN ACADEMY MURDERS
13: THE THREE-MINUTE UNIVERSE
14: *STAR TREK*: THE MOTION PICTURE
15: *STAR TREK*: THE WRATH OF KHAN
16: MEMORY PRIME
17: THE ENTROPY EFFECT
18: THE FINAL NEXUS
19: THE WOUNDED SKY
20: VULCAN'S GLORY
21: MY ENEMY, MY ALLY
22: DOUBLE, DOUBLE
23: THE COVENANT OF THE CROWN
24: CORONA
25: THE ABODE OF LIFE
26: ISHMAEL
27: WEB OF THE ROMULANS
28: CRY OF THE ONLIES
Coming soon:
29: DREADNOUGHT

STAR TREK: *THE NEXT GENERATION* NOVELS

0: ENCOUNTER AT FARPOINT
1: GHOST SHIP
2: THE PEACEKEEPERS
3: THE CHILDREN OF HAMLIN
4: SURVIVORS
5: STRIKE ZONE
6: POWER HUNGRY
7: MASKS
8: THE CAPTAIN'S HONOUR
Coming soon:
9: A CALL TO DARKNESS

STAR TREK GIANT NOVELS

STRANGERS FROM THE SKY
FINAL FRONTIER
UHURA'S SONG
DWELLERS IN THE CRUCIBLE

STAR TREK LARGE FORMAT

MR. SCOTT'S GUIDE TO THE ENTERPRISE
THE *STAR TREK* COMPENDIUM
THE *STAR TREK* INTERVIEW BOOK
THE WORLDS OF THE FEDERATION

A *STAR TREK*® NOVEL

THE CRY OF THE ONLIES
JUDY KLASS

TITAN BOOKS
LONDON

STAR TREK 28: THE CRY OF THE ONLIES
ISBN 1 85286 210 6

Published by
Titan Books Ltd
58 St Giles High St
London WC2H 8LH

First Titan Edition October 1989
10 9 8 7 6 5 4 3 2 1

British edition by arrangement with Pocket Books, a division of
Simon & Schuster, Inc., Under Exclusive License from
Paramount Pictures Corporation, The Trademark Owner.

Printed and bound in Great Britain by Cox and Wyman Ltd,
Reading, Berkshire.

For Mom and Pop

ACKNOWLEDGMENTS

There are a number of people I would like to acknowledge:

The awful people I went to Paris with in 1987; had they not been so awful, I would not have wandered off to the Gare de Lyon and started scribbling this novel in my notebook.

I would like to thank Karen ("Kasey") Carrillo for telling me to get motivated.

Sam Bacon was right about *some* things, after all.

A number of friends read copies of the manuscript in various stages. I would like to thank Colin Edwards, Tricia Dailey, Patty French, Nicholas Jenks, Tom Adshead, and Alexandra de Brito for their interest and helpful suggestions.

I also want to thank Jean Arbeiter and my agent, Herb Katz, for their support.

Historian's Note

This adventure takes place during the U.S.S. *Enterprise's* initial five-year mission, sometime after the events chronicled in the television episodes "Miri" and "Requiem for Methuselah." The reader may wish to consult those episodes as referents.

Prologue

A HEARTBEAT IN DARKNESS. The cold of metal, the warmth of his own arms, hugging himself. Pal lay with his head tucked down, his knees pressed up against his chest, and shivered in the cold of the storage compartment. A strange foolie. He would disappear.

He could hear Jahn out in the big room, with the lights and the buzzing knobs, and the picture of the spiral snake of green light going round and round. And the big screen, crammed full of stars, and deep, dark scary night.

Jahn was yelling crazy things. He had yelled at Pal, until Pal crawled away when he wasn't looking and hid in the storage compartment. Had yelled that he was helping Pal and Rhea—saving them from the Grups. Pal hadn't said anything. Didn't say that Jahn looked to him like a Grup, looked and acted and sounded like a Grup, except without some of the nice things. Grups could be nice, sometimes.

It was scary in the storage compartment; someone might open the door and find him.

Oh, and so why don't you hide in the other room?

I can't, they might see me go, I've got to stay here, now.

Well, why didn't you hide there before?

I'm scared of there, because there are no Onlies there, and maybe there are snakes, and I'm scared of snakes.

Why, have you been bad?

Yes, I think I have been bad, and when you are bad, the snakes come.

Pal rocked back and forth and made noises like a small bird. Exactly like a certain small gray-brown bird. He had learned how long ago. Very long ago.

Sometimes Rhea went into the other room, and then it was safe, and there were no snakes. Pal liked to be in there with her. They would play some of the old games; it made everything seem more normal. And she would sing a song to him that Miri used to sing, and he would be able to sleep. It was a very nice song, and it went like this:

> Lumpkin, pumpkin, let me show you something,
> Trick or a foolie, burn down the school, he
> Ran to the doctor, doctor had a chopper,
> Ran through the town, and the Grups fell down . . .

Pal liked this song, and the Grups had said they liked it too. They had had Miri sing it into a machine that recorded her voice, and then Miri didn't want to sing it anymore.

Where's Miri?

I don't know, something bad happened to her.

What happened to her?

Shut up, stop it, you'll make the snakes come.

The voice in Pal's head that talked to him was not

Pal's voice. It used to be somebody else's voice in the white room with the cold light and the hard chair, but somehow the voice was in his head now, and it didn't like him, and it gobbled him up, until he curled away, like a kernel in a nutshell. He used to be so fast once, and run, and giggle, and fight sometimes, but now he looked for dark cracks and caves, and curled up like a ball inside them. He was getting bigger, but he felt little. He wanted to fade away into the air, get tinier and tinier and wink out, like a baby, growing backward.

Rhea, he remembered, used to be a little Only. But now she seemed big, and she acted like the ones who had always been big, acted like Miri or Jahn or Louise. Why did she seem different? She wore her hair up now. "Ponytail." And Jahn had always been big, and he still was, but now he seemed kind of mean, like Grups in the Before Time were supposed to be, the burning, hurting Grups. *Doctor had a chopper . . . the Grups fell down . . .*

Sometimes it seemed like maybe Jahn didn't know the right thing to do. Before, for all the time there was, Jahn had known what was right. He and the other big Onlies had led and explained the world. Jahn could run fastest, bounce a bird with one rock, melt into walls in the hiding game, punish clowns in the circus foolie. Pal had wanted so much to be like him. But the new Grups treated Jahn like he was little. Lots of Onlies didn't listen to him anymore. They did what the Grups said, instead. How could he and Rhea have changed so much? How come Pal saw them as different? He used to believe in Jahn, and in the ways of the Onlies, before the Grups came back.

The sound of Jahn yelling came filtering through to

11

Pal, with a metallic echo. Yelling at Rhea? Or just yelling? Jahn was playing the Starfleet foolie.

"I'm the captain of this ship! I give the orders. Shields up! Drop them on my signal, and fire main phaser banks!"

"Jahn, we have no shields, there's no need to fire the phasers. But please keep an eye on the air pressure monitor. And the cloaking device . . ."

That was Rhea's voice. She was there.

Jahn cut her off. "Don't argue with me, Lieutenant! I run a tight ship, you follow my orders." Then, in a more nervous voice, "Where's Pal?"

Fear knotted Pal's stomach at the thought of being sought out and discovered. Oh, why hadn't he gone to the other room?

"I don't know, Jahn. I think he's hiding. I think maybe you're scaring him. Try to be calmer. Just let me have the controls for a moment . . ."

"I'm hungry."

"There's soup and stuff. I programmed it in the computer. Just punch for it."

Pal could hear them moving, shuffling past the compartment in which he lay hidden. His hand suddenly felt something in the corner of the compartment, something he had never touched, never known was there before. A coiled wire, like a snake, like the snake on the spiral viewscreen that went round and round, lay on the closet floor beside Pal. It felt slippery and cold. He shuddered.

In the main cabin, the food computer hummed, and then beeped. Pal heard it. He was hungry too. Grup food was better than Only food had ever been. He hoped that there would be some left for him.

Maybe the Grups would come, and make things all right, and then he could crawl out of the storage closet.

Oh, and what if they are mad at you?

I'll say sorry, I'll try to be good now. And if they don't want me, then I'll die . . . he would do anything they wanted, to make it better.

Maybe the Onlies and the others who got hurt would get better, and Miri would be there and Dr. Nazafar-7, and things would be okay. The blood and the screaming would be gone from the Home World. And the snakes. He wished he hadn't gone with Jahn and Rhea. He wasn't sure why he had, exactly. It had all happened so fast, been so scary.

Some of the Grups were scary. But he liked Mrs. File and Dr. Colignon. And Dr. Nazafar-7. He hoped they would still like him. Maybe Jahn and Rhea would be glad to see the Grups too. He wished someone would find them.

Chapter One

Captain's Log, Stardate 6118.2:

The *Enterprise* is en route to the planet Boaco Six. Our mission: to contact the rebel government of this world and try to smooth relations between its ruling council and the Federation. At the same time, we must be alert to signs of Klingon infiltration and report on the extent of both Klingon and Romulan influence in this system.

KIRK FLICKED OFF the switch on the arm of his captain's chair with a certain weariness. On the main screen ahead of him, the twelve-planet system of Boaco grew steadily in size. Boaco Eight was inhabited and was a Federation ally, but it was not the reason they had come. There would be no stopover there, this time.

With a deft touch of his control panel, Helmsman Sulu brought the sixth planet of the system clearly into focus. All three of the planet's lunar satellites were visible from the starship's angle of approach. It was a small planet, warmed by the twin Boacan suns, maroon and orange and black when viewed from space.

"Mr. Chekov, drop to one-half impulse. Set standard orbit."

"Aye, sir." Chekov carried out the order.

At his science station, Spock took the tape of the most recent Federation-issued report on Boaco Six and fed it into the computer. He read aloud the information that appeared on his screen.

"Boaco Six. Class M planet. Population approximately three million inhabitants. Three lunar satellites. Planet of exceeding beauty, lush vegetation, zoological diversity.

"For centuries, the two great landmasses have been ruled by a series of corrupt and ruthless warlords. Their rule was overthrown two years ago by a planetwide revolution. The rebels are known to have received substantial military aid from the Klingons, to have bought seafaring vessels and primitive flying machines from the Romulans, and dilithium crystals from the planet Orion.

"The good relations the Federation maintained with several of the warlords of Boaco Six caused the rebel rulers, the so-called Council of Youngers, to distrust the Federation of Planets and rally the population against it. And once in power, the rebels immediately severed all ties with the Federation.

"As a political and military stronghold, Boaco Six would be of great value to the Klingons and the Romulans. The rebels are greatly feared by the planet of Boaco Eight, the only other habitable world in the system, which alarmed by signs that the sixth planet may be building a space fleet, seeks Federation protection."

Spock paused and straightened before his science panel. "The report continues, Captain, with random facts and minutiae about the geographical makeup of this world. Do you wish me to read it?"

"No, Mr. Spock, thank you. That's enough for now."

Everyone on the bridge, and in fact everyone on the *Enterprise* whose service might somehow be called upon during this mission, had already read this report and studied the Boacan situation. But a restatement of the facts just before contact was made was standard Federation procedure, and, Kirk reflected, good common sense. Still, he knew that official reports on the planet did not discuss every aspect of its case; much was left out, or could be read between the lines.

He had mixed feelings about this mission. And less than his usual enthusiasm about his role. True, Boaco Six promised to be an exciting world, one of great beauty, famous for its food, music, friendly inhabitants, and cultural traditions. After the general overhaul on Starbase Twelve, and a protracted series of war games with smaller Starfleet vessels, Kirk felt contact with an exotic, less advanced world would be good for him and his crew. Exploration could be more therapeutic than shore leave. They might see some hands-on action after such a long period of inactivity and escape from the pressures of dealing with the Klingons or the Romulans for a while.

But did Boaco Six really offer any such escape? Or only more of the same? It was those very galactic pressures, after all, that caused the *Enterprise* to glide through space into this solar system. One false move by the planet's rulers, and it could easily become the nexus of the conflict. If they *were* involved with the Klingons—and it was likely they were—Starfleet strategy would dictate that their world be seen as a very expendable chess piece in the larger game.

It was a tricky game, but one Kirk knew how to play. *We'll do whatever is required. I could work up a little more enthusiasm, though, if our position were a little better defined. If we were a little more clearly on the side of 'Right' in this one, whatever skulduggery is required to win.*

Doubt soured, somewhat, the anticipation of adventure. The Federation had not always handled this solar system wisely. Kirk felt that it now fell to him to unknot an entanglement dating back decades or more. It was not the first time he'd had such a feeling.

The young guard on duty by the door of the turbolift felt none of his captain's weariness or ambivalence. For him the strain in galactic relations was not so much an ominous crisis as a test, a personal challenge, a game he had arrived just in time to take part in. It frightened him, exhilarated him. He was new on the bridge, and stood perhaps *too* stiffly at attention at his post, but his eyes darted round him at the men and women on the bridge, all busy with their jobs, as if he could not quite accept that he was there with them. He jumped as the captain addressed him.

"Ensign Michaels. You've studied the Boaco Six situation in-depth, as you'll be accompanying us on this mission. I'd like to hear your opinion. How would you appraise our role?"

The guard, who had first heard of Kirk at the Academy as of a semimythical figure, whose name was invoked admiringly by teachers and cadets alike, tried to conceal his nervousness as he replied. He had hardly ever spoken to the captain, but for the casual welcome aboard when he signed on. He sought to give him a sure, hard answer now.

"Sir, I think diplomacy is of secondary importance here. Our priority is not to coax these people out of

17

their belligerence. We've got to take a firm stand, let them know the Federation is not to be flouted or made a fool of, that we *know* which side they're on . . ."

"Our mission is to investigate that, Ensign, *and* to establish relations, if possible," Kirk said gently.

"With all due respect, sir, we can't deal too lightly in a situation like this." Michaels spoke with all the conviction of inexperience. "We owe it to Boaco Eight, and the small systems in this quadrant that depend on us, to take a strong stand."

"Thank you, Ensign," Kirk said. "But for the moment, I think we'll watch and listen, and play it by ear."

Michaels did not reply, but it was obvious from his expression that he considered his captain's plan of action too casual, too cavalier.

You can read everything he's thinking, Kirk mused. *They should have a special course at the Academy, to teach these kids how to maintain a poker face. Speaking of which . . .*

"Mr. Spock. You'll accompany me on this mission. It seems delicate enough to require both of us. Dr. McCoy will come as well. Notify him and call Mr. Scott to the bridge to assume command." Kirk rose from his chair and moved toward the turbolift. "Lieutenant Uhura, the ruling council on this planet has some kind of primitive radio, doesn't it?"

"Yes, sir. They've contacted Federation ships before, if only to taunt them and send political slogans."

"Try to hail them and tell them we'll be beaming down."

Uhura punched in an intergalactic salute and decoded the response which came feebly crackling back. "They say they don't wish to communicate with you directly now, sir. But they promise to receive you in their council chamber and guarantee your safety. I'll feed the coordinates for beam-down to the transporter room."

"Very good, Lieutenant. Landing party will assemble in the transporter room in ten minutes."

Kirk left the bridge.

Chapter Two

"I DON'T LIKE IT," McCoy grumbled, as they assembled on the transporter platform. "A guarantee of safety from some renegade government. *That's* enough for you and Spock to risk your necks on the same mission?"

Kirk grinned. "Not to mention yours, eh, Bones?"

"That's right, not to mention mine!" McCoy growled.

Kirk had actually had a similar thought and included two security guards in the landing party at the last minute. Michaels stared at them resentfully; they seemed to guarantee less of a role for him. But Kirk knew that in a real confrontation, their party would still have a disadvantage. And you're never so vulnerable as you are directly after you beam down. His eyes flicked to Spock, serene, a few feet away from him, whose hand hovered near the phaser strapped to his waist. Always standing close by him, like a shadow of steel.

Kirk straightened on the transporter pad. "Energize," he said.

It was night on the side of the planet where they rematerialized. They reoriented themselves and saw that there was no hostile force waiting to attack them or to take them hostage. In fact, there seemed to be no one there to meet them at all.

"Efficient, well-run world," McCoy said sarcastically.

"Belay that, Bones. They don't have transporters, yet. Let's hope they know what they're doing and gave us the right coordinates." Kirk eased open his communicator. "Mr. Scott?"

"Aye, Captain. Everything all right down there?"

"So far, Scotty, as far as we can tell. We may have to transport again, though, so stand by. Kirk out."

The night air was rich and cool. The jungle around them rustled and buzzed with night-insect and animal noises. Two of the planet's three moons could be seen hanging in the sky through an orange mist. With two suns and three moons, it could never become truly dark here, Kirk reflected. Or cold.

The underbrush they began picking their way through was wet, red and maroon in color, and the ground was soft and shadowed, and squished beneath their boots. Spock's tricorder whirred.

"We are several miles from the ocean, Captain. And there is a primitive city less than a kilometer due south."

This last announcement was not really necessary. They could hear and smell this center of activity, as music, smoke, and the aroma of roasting animals came faintly filtering through to them, over and through the bending trees and hanging vines.

There was a spring in Kirk's step; he felt light and relaxed. Could the strain and worry of the last few weeks have dispersed so rapidly? More likely, he thought, it was this planet's small size and weaker gravitational pull that made him feel so lighthearted. Earth was larger, and the gravity simulation unit on the *Enterprise* made for a stronger pull than this.

McCoy caught his sleeve on a double-pronged blackthorn, and swore as a lizardlike creature darted its tongue out at him round a tree trunk and disappeared into a hole in the rough purple bark. "Crazy Federation cloak-and-dagger diplomacy! *This* is an important world? So backward they can't even manage a road to the city?"

"I think there is one. We're just slightly off the mark." Kirk smiled. "Don't worry, Bones. You read the reports. None of the animals or plants are poisonous."

"You mean none are *lethal*," the doctor grumbled. "There are many poison pills a man has to swallow that won't kill him."

"Indeed, Doctor," Spock said. "And after the unpleasant barrage of pills and inoculations you gave us on board, I should think we are all well protected against anything short of an avalanche."

McCoy did not deign to respond.

Complain as he might, Kirk knew that the doctor would have been hurt and disappointed if he had not been included on the mission. There had been reports of incredible advances in jungle medicine made by the rebel government, the coordination of programs of inoculation, hospital building, and geriatric care, all of which McCoy wanted to investigate firsthand.

Spock held his tricorder close to the trunks of the

22

tall, winding trees as they passed. "As expected, Captain. These trees contain high concentrations of the chemical argea. This forest is a veritable gold mine for chemical developers.

"*And* doctors," McCoy put in.

"Argea?" Ensign Michaels said. "Does that come from this planet? I don't remember it being mentioned in the report."

"It doesn't have to be mentioned, boy," McCoy said gruffly. "Everyone knows that Boaco Six has supplied the Federation with raw argea for over a century. Or at least they did until two years ago. Naturally, they stopped selling it when the revolution came along. But Federation interest in this world started way back when scientists discovered how argea could be used to keep the human heart and spleen healthy."

"There is a sad irony to the situation," Spock commented. "The precious argea brought little profit to the Boacans themselves. Only to the foreign companies who purchased it and would strip and destroy whole forests for it. And since the chemical was processed far from their planet, it is one of the many medical supplies they have never had."

"That's why the revolution came as such a shock to the Federation," Kirk said. "There are other planets that have argea-producing plants. None sell it as readily or as cheaply as Boaco Six used to. But once the revolutionary council took power, they sent the companies from the other stars packing."

Michaels frowned and shook his head. "Seems too important for the report not to have mentioned it," he said at last.

Kirk wondered if young men were getting younger,

or if it was just his imagination. *Even if the kid was a math whiz and did so brilliantly at the Academy, they shouldn't have given him to me half-green.*

Michaels had not spent much time on any intermediate vessels. A well-liked and hardworking student at the Academy, he had struggled to live up to the flash of genius he had shown in early childhood, and convinced his teachers of his precocity. He had been sent almost fresh upon this, his first tour of duty on a starship. Though he'd been on board for only a week, Kirk had decided to include him on the mission. The life of an ensign was one of tedium and drudgery, a round of stints at guard duty, the cleaning and maintenance of machinery, emergency practice drills, and perhaps busywork in the labs or gardens. Normally, months would go by before Michaels's name would come up on a mission roster.

But when a crewman first came aboard, Kirk liked to include him quickly on one important, exciting mission, as a taste of things to come. As the ancients had let children begin their studies with a taste of honey, licked off the page. It had been the policy of his own first starship captain, Captain Garrovick, and was one he had followed.

The shadowy leaves under the orange night sky billowed and waved. Suddenly, one of the shadows came alive. Something large, furry, and rodentlike leapt down from a low-hanging branch with a screech and wrapped itself around Kirk's neck. Its legs were tipped with what had seemed, as it moved through the air, to be distended claws, but as they touched Kirk's skin they seemed to be clammy toes, spongy soft and clinging, like suction cups.

"Captain!" The cry broke from Spock, packed with tight concern, anxiety kept barely in check.

"Jim, get it off!" McCoy yelled.

Kirk sank his hands into the creature's mangy fur, and pulled. But its grip was firm—it seemed attached to the skin of his throat and shoulder. It smelled damp and rank. He could not see its head, it was brushing and rooting along his forehead. Although he knew his life was not in danger, he prayed that it had no stinger. Or sharp teeth.

"What do you want us to do, sir?" Michaels cried, his voice almost hysterical.

At last, Kirk pried the creature loose and hurled its fat body down into the underbrush. One of the security guards, who had been hovering, anxiously watching, now whipped out his phaser and blasted the creature full force. A white beam shot out, the small feral body glowed and lit up the ground, then vanished into air. The ground around it was sunken, the foliage charred.

Kirk was shaken by the attack, but he frowned at the guard. "Easy, Thorton. There was no need for that. Everyone—phasers on stun. Especially now, as we enter the city."

He was surprisingly rattled, and very glad that their group was moving out of the forest. Sap and twigs clung to his hair. Every leaf, vine, and tree now seemed to bristle with life; the eyes of small animals peered through the shadows that traced the edges of the semidarkness. But animal noises were giving way to human ones, to the sounds of laughter and music.

"Do you think we're walking into a trap, Captain?" asked Michaels.

"No, Ensign," Kirk shook his head. "Just into a very noisy town."

The foliage around them grew smaller and less dense, and finally parted into a clearing. A mud road snaked around from the opposite direction, turning to brick as it ran before the buildings of the settlement, a hodgepodge of thatched huts, stone and brick houses, and rickety-looking taller buildings of stone and metal. Rising in several places above the other rooftops were monumental structures of a white stone, like marble, ornamented with pillars and statuaries. These buildings were torn and gutted—the reminders of a fallen regime.

There were roasting pits in the streets, each in front of a cluster of the smaller houses, and in each pit there was a fire with a spit and a roasting animal. The meat smelled good. Women basted it with sauce. They turned it with knives, double-pronged like the jungle thorns. But one could see that, whatever animal was being cooked, it had six legs, three on each side, as the carcasses turned on their spits. Kirk felt an instinctive revulsion at the eating of non-four-legged animals that all his interplanetary travels had not cured him of. Lord knew what Spock, from a planet of vegetarians, felt.

The security guards, who brought up the rear, became more watchful as the landing party entered the moving mass of people. Children with unwashed faces and tattered clothing shrieked and chased each other, and tumbled underfoot. Their parents eyed the strangers cautiously but did not call the children away or hide them indoors. They obviously remembered the Federation uniform and did not consider it one to fear. *At least they haven't been brainwashed to that extent,* Kirk thought.

One grizzled old man, at their approach, pulled off a thin, leathery belt with inlaid stones and a metal clasp. He waved it in the air and called out, "Hey!

Spacemen! Look! Come buy authentic artifact, with ethnic design, made by native of Boaco Six."

His neighbors laughed. Spock raised a questioning eyebrow, and the landing party moved on.

"Sarcasm, Captain?"

"Maybe he was serious. Since the revolution and the break with the Federation, I'd imagine there's been quite a falling off on the tourist trade."

As they walked on, many people smiled at them, and waved.

"You see that, Spock?" McCoy said. "Even with all the tension between their world and ourselves? You see the kindness and neighborliness of ordinary folks?"

Spock appeared unmoved by his goading and did not respond.

"That's the saving grace of the galaxy, really," McCoy continued reflectively, innocently. "The simple homey virtues that so often go unrewarded. Warmth and friendship, given freely to strangers, *gratis.*" He stared off, as if pondering this point.

Spock, at last, raised a bemused eyebrow. "Indeed, Doctor? Your great emotionalism and sentimentality tell you so. But logic would indicate that the local people are glad to see us for the reasons the captain just mentioned—for the promise of tourist trade and industry our presence seems to bring."

"Humph. So I'm overly emotional and sentimental, am I?" the doctor demanded.

"Unquestionably."

"Well, amen to that," McCoy said emphatically.

"Gentlemen, gentlemen," Kirk said, and smiled.

Local nightlife seemed easy and pleasant. Girls leaned out of windows on their elbows and chatted with young men. Families were sharing their meals in groups, children tearing messily at the meat; some were skeletal, grossly underfed. Many of the women and a few of the men wore the rich embroidered native garb. Others, especially the children, wore torn and soiled suits from the Federated Planets, designed for the wild, of strange synthetic cloths manufactured far from their world. And one little girl, playing a game by herself, something like marbles, wore a dress of obviously Klingon design and make.

"Captain, look! That kid's jumper . . ."

"I see her, Michaels. But we need to concentrate on reaching this Council of Youngers."

"I suggest, Captain, that the council chamber may be housed there," Spock said, pointing to one of the gutted ornate white buildings. A guard was posted around it.

"Remember, keep cool," Kirk urged his men softly. They headed for the building, past a sagging metal-and-wood structure covered with moss and hanging vines. It seemed to be some sort of tavern. Men and women were laughing and talking inside, and drinking. Probably that black sparkling Boacan brandy, Kirk thought, rare and expensive in any other quadrant. There had been a two-year embargo.

"Well, at any rate, Federation reports of oppression and starvation under the rulers seem to have been exaggerated," McCoy remarked drily.

"This isn't the whole world. This may be a model area they wish us to see." Kirk would form no firm opinions until he spoke to the council.

They ascended the soiled and crumbling steps of the old building. Beneath the arch of its doorway, two guards, a boy and a girl, armed with crude firearms, suddenly appeared and aimed at them. Both were about sixteen years old, wearing expressions of fierce pride. With a slight motion of his hand, Kirk indicated to his own men that they were not to draw.

"We're here by invitation," he said mildly, "to see the Council of Youngers of Boaco Six. Could you conduct us to them?"

The young man nodded. "I can. But first, you must give us your weapons."

Kirk considered for a moment and then gave the order to comply, against McCoy's sputtering. They followed the boy and the girl down the hall, the security guards looking foolish and uneasy as only security guards deprived of their phasers can.

Massive wood doors rose before them.

"Wait here," the girl said, and disappeared through one of them, in her arms a harvest of phasers. The boy stood guard, his crude gun still trained on the men of the *Enterprise. Playing soldier,* Kirk thought. *But this revolution has half the kids on the planet in on the game.*

The girl reappeared a moment later and eased open the creaking, elaborately carved doors.

"Tamara Angel will see you now," she said.

Chapter Three

THE OPEN DOORS revealed a large, high-ceilinged chamber. A long wooden table ran down the center of it. And sitting on the table was a young woman.

"Come in, gentlemen. Take a seat," she said.

Kirk chose a chair a few feet away from her, and his men filed in behind him and sat down. Tamara Angel pivoted to face them, hugging her knees up to her chest. She, too, was surprisingly young. She wore a military uniform. Her long black hair was coiled in a neat bun at the nape of her neck. Her radiant face wore an expression of amusement and confidence. Her boots beat a tattoo on the table.

"So, after arming our oppressors, and seeking to sabotage our revolution and our government, the beneficent Federation of Planets has decided to contact us. Which of you is called Captain Kirk?"

Kirk rose. "I'm Captain James T. Kirk of the Starship *Enterprise*. We come in good faith, acknowledging that there have been differences between us, but in the hope that we can reach an understanding."

"You come to spy. And to manufacture propaganda for the Federation, which would have the galaxy think it means to deal fairly with us."

"Miss Angel . . ."

"You may call me Tamara." She flashed a mischievous smile, which Kirk could not penetrate. He instinctively knew that his own considerable ability to charm would be of no use here.

"Tamara." He decided to adopt a more authoritative tone. "As I say, we have come in good faith, and expected to be conducted to the ruling council of this planet. Instead, we were beamed down to an obscure area, found our way here on our own, and would now appreciate an interview with your superiors."

"I have no superiors," she replied blandly. "In the council we are all on equal footing. I am the minister of interplanetary relations. Whatever message the Federation has given you, you can relay to me."

"What other ministers are there?"

She sighed and counted on her fingers. "Minister of health, minister of public welfare, minister of relations with Boaco Eight, minister of finance, minister of justice, minister of education, minister of religion . . . we may create more if new situations call for it."

"And, of course, you're all elected very democratically, once you 'create' these ministries for yourselves," McCoy interjected.

Tamara Angel's face became harder. "We are leading our planet out of a time of chaos and war. Healing factions. Mobilizing massive drives against illiteracy, disease, crop failure, rabid animals, starvation. There is little time for us to go on the campaign trail." The sly smile returned. "Besides. The people of Boaco Six are used to old-style government. Like that of your old

31

friends, Anator, Markor, and Puil, our former rulers who you did such good business with. No one here has yet heard of democracy. Perhaps sometime soon they will learn, and we can have elections."

"Once you've brainwashed them all to support you!" Michaels burst out. The ensign was out of line, but Kirk did not rebuke him. After all, protocol never stopped McCoy from putting in his two cents.

It was Spock, who had been sitting beside Kirk silently, who now steered the conversation in a more constructive direction. He rose. "Tamara. You accuse us of spying. Yet the only way we can possibly build trust and understanding is if you let us learn more about you. It would do your government no harm if you let us observe the changes you have made that you are so proud of."

Tamara Angel gave a curt nod. "Yes. We let you beam down to the outskirts of our city so that you could get a sense of the people of Boaco Six. This is our capital city, Boa. It is the largest city on this landmass. You may think it primitive, but it sprawls on for miles. Our people are changing, rebuilding it.

"To your Federation, our planet is just another number, another galactic pawn. A source of argea and other raw materials. To understand us, you must see how old and complex our culture is. And at the same time, how young we are. This is a revolution of youth. You see, for centuries"—she became tight-lipped, then continued—"the life expectancy here has not been very high. We are hoping to change that. But for now, it is a world for the young. Only the young can reshape an entire planet. Because they do not know the rules, they reinvent them."

Kirk was impressed by the intelligence and conviction with which she challenged him. The seeming irreverence she brought to affairs of state was matched by an absolute belief in the justice of her cause.

"Well, Captain," she said, "would you be willing to take the risk of hearing us out, learning our point of view?"

"We're eager to learn more about you. Perhaps a meeting with the entire council can be arranged?"

"You will meet more of the ministers tomorrow. They will show you around. And perhaps, in a few days, we can all meet together, yes?"

Kirk had instructions to spend as much as a week here, if it seemed advisable. The planet was so crucial, the issues in which it was involved so complex. "That makes sense," he said.

Spock observed his captain as they were escorted by the boy guard to a nearby bungalow to spend the night. A squat, ungainly building, it was covered with a matted thatch of leaves, which spilled down from the roof, along the outer walls. Once inside, Kirk scanned the room with his eyes, and stretched. He checked in with Mr. Scott, and with satisfaction tried the bolt on the door. He gave the impression of nonchalance, but Spock knew him well enough to detect a quiet uneasiness, doubtless due to the lack of phasers. Kirk felt his men were too vulnerable. Of course, he could have had new ones beamed down from the *Enterprise,* if only just for the night. The Boacans would never know. Yet Spock knew that Kirk would never do this. It would violate the captain's peculiar elaborate personal code of honor to do so; he wanted to win the Boacans' trust, and so could not even hoodwink them in secrecy.

McCoy was the one officially in charge of looking after the captain's physical and mental well-being. Yet for Spock, too, Kirk's health and state of mind were extremely important. Any danger or disturbance that Kirk fell victim to played upon the Vulcan's nerves as if they were harp strings. He knew he was too vigilant; worry was a contemptible human emotion. He rationalized it; after all, had he not used all his years among humans to study them, to try to understand the way they thought? And was not Jim Kirk an especially fine and complex human to observe, embodying every facet of the standard Terran personality, only much more so?

As first officer, was it not *his* official duty, as well as McCoy's, to be certain at all times that the captain was fit and safe and functioning at his best? Also, he reasoned, the empathy between his captain and himself was especially strong because a wisp of empathy always hangs between a telepath and one to whose mind he has been linked. And Spock had mindmelded with his captain on several occasions.

Spock watched Kirk now, watched him smoothly allay the fears of his men, so that they could relax and go to sleep. Young Michaels was haranguing him, in a manner which seemed to Spock a severe breach of discipline. Kirk checked the boy, gently but firmly. So confident was he about his position of command that he could keep the atmosphere loose and informal. *The difference between us,* thought Spock, who in command situations always went by the book.

"Why let *her* tell us what to do, Captain? Why let them deal with us so casually? It's so obvious that they deliberately set out to insult us. They must know how much is at stake here. They're testing us."

"I don't think an insult was intended, Michaels. They have no idea how to conduct these affairs. They're soldiers, not diplomats," Kirk said approvingly.

"But can't you see . . ."

"I *can't* see any point in discussing it further, Ensign. Get some sleep. I need you alert tomorrow, and with an open mind."

The security guards had the beds nearest the door. They asked the captain if they should take turns staying awake and standing guard. Kirk gave them a negative, told them to turn in. Spock thought it likely that he would order them to beam back up to the *Enterprise* in the morning. *Jim seems to instinctively like this place, seems very relaxed here. Perhaps, after all, too relaxed.* Fresh air, the warm night, the rich smell of the floor of the bungalow could, Spock knew, ease a human's guard, make him too trusting. There was a tendency among humans to see a planet at an early stage of development as a paradise: free, protective, and unspoilt. Such thinking was irrational. It was a thing to be watched against.

But the jingoism of Michaels was indeed trying. He lay on his cot, whispering, still arguing, spouting a line of thought currently very popular among Starfleet Academy cadets. "The Klingons *have* no final goal, they're insatiable, they'll stop at nothing. And little worlds like this, they don't know what they're doing, don't know what they're letting themselves in for. They buy arms from the Klingons—might as well sell their souls to the devil. Whatever problems there were here, whatever the old rulers were like, they must have been better than the new ones; these people are beyond our reasoning and beyond our help. They think they're fighting for freedom, and then their whole world will turn into a prison camp, and it happens over and over . . ."

The two security guards listened and nodded solemnly.

McCoy flicked a beetle off his blanket and propped himself up on one elbow. "What do you think of all this, Spock?"

"Of the new Boacan regime, Doctor? It is much too early to form a concrete opinion. What I have seen so far has struck me as positive."

The three young men, who conceived of the stoic Spock as the most conservative of officers, were obviously surprised to hear him speak this way.

"You think this revolution will turn out to be a good thing, sir?" Michaels asked.

"I didn't say that, Ensign. But I understand the scale of the ugliness and evil that were here before. The brutality, the waste, the utter disregard for life. And I understand the impulse to replace that bitter reality. No more can be said at this time."

Kirk lifted the large orange candle lighting the bungalow from its rickety table and blew it out.

"And with that, men, let's get some sleep."

Chapter Four

THE SECURITY GUARDS did return to the ship in the morning. An agricultural specialist, an expert in jungle education, and a historian were beamed down to replace them. The phasers were returned, which seemed a show of good faith on the part of Tamara Angel. A breakfast of meat was provided, with a separate bowl of fruit for Spock, apparently because of his Vulcan vegetarian beliefs. This, to Kirk, also seemed surprisingly knowing and thoughtful.

After the meal, Kirk found Spock outside the bungalow, watching the city come alive. Merchants and women selling fruit were taking to the streets, rhythmically wailing out praise of their goods. Small, reptilian flying creatures, with ridiculous feathery tufts on their heads, swooped between buildings, and picked at bits of meat that had dropped off the spits of the night before. And small lizards crept in the dust along the roadside, their backs the rich orange color of the dust in which they lived.

"Fascinating, isn't it, Captain?" Spock said, pointing at various creatures. "These reptilelike birds, and these dust lizards, are animals which have become fully adapted to urban life, dependent on it, as rats and pigeons and sparrows and some insects were, at one time, on your Earth. And look at that animal," he continued, indicating a scruffy snout which poked through the doorway of a house across the road from them. "In the wild, it is remarkable for its intelligence *and* its ferocity. But the Boacans have managed to tame them, and domesticate them, and they are fiercely loyal, ideal for guarding homes. Almost no household is without one. Unfortunately, many of the local animals are inedible, which is why starvation has sometimes been a problem—though usually not in times of peace. And look at *that* beast of burden carrying that tinsmith's pots." Spock switched his focus once again. "It carries its young in a pouch, similar to marsupials on Earth, and to Denebian momruks. But this does not impede its usefulness to merchants here."

Kirk squinted lazily at the ungainly shabby creature as it rolled its fleshy body along, close to the ground, and clattered with its pots and pans down the street. It was followed by a young boy who carried a large pole.

"One must admit, Captain," Spock went on, "that the variety of fauna on this planet is striking and impressive. Even here, in the heart of the capital city. And because of the incompetence of the old rulers, and our bad relations with the new ones, it has never been properly cataloged."

"Remember, Mr. Spock," Kirk said, "we're not here on a zoological expedition. We've got plenty of other things to be looking into."

"Quite so, Captain. I was merely struck by the abundance of uncharted wildlife around us."

The light from the two suns poured down and lit the clay and wooden walls of the buildings, which were covered with a film of morning dew. The moisture was black, but it lit up as brilliant fuchsia when penetrated by sunlight. One of the three moons still hung in the early morning air, a sliver, silvery pale.

"Yes, this place is remarkable," Kirk said slowly. "A tragedy that violence has marred it for so long."

The sounds of infants crying and of sleepy children waking and chattering could be heard in the neighboring homes. A woman five houses away came into her yard to shake out a blanket, and shooed away the reptile birds feasting on scraps. They descended again when she was gone. The tufts on their heads hung over their beaks as they plucked at the dust.

"There's something invigorating about a world like this, Spock. Something renewing."

Kirk's beatific expression as he said this caused Spock to express his concerns of the night before. "And yet, Captain, a deceptively lovely atmosphere could alter our perceptions, interfere with our investigations."

Kirk smiled. "Don't worry, Mr. Spock. I'm more taken by the return of our phasers than by the pretty scenery." He felt the butt of the phaser reassuringly strapped at his hip. "That girl, Tamara Angel . . ."

"An unusual minister of state."

"Most definitely. Do you think 'Angel' is a family name, Spock? Or a name she's taken for herself?"

"A combination of both, Captain. History tapes show that the Angel family is an old and prestigious one on Boaco Six. The real name is ancient and, to a Terran tongue, unpronounceable. 'Angel' is an attractive English rendering of it."

Kirk knew that his first officer's own Vulcan family

name was something equally impossible to pronounce. But there was no such colorful English version of it. "Well, if the rest of the ministers are like her, we're in for quite a week."

They reentered the bungalow. The recomposed landing party was assembled, its new members briefed. A young boy guard appeared in the doorway, to escort them to a nearby public square to meet the minister of education. His name was Noro. He pumped their hands eagerly, an impossibly young, slightly awkward fellow who was missing many of his teeth. Kirk tried to imagine this unprepossessing youth shouldering the job of educating a world whose illiteracy rate had always been staggeringly high.

After introductions were completed, nine lumbering animals were led into the public square on tethers. They were covered with gray fur, short and downy as peach fuzz, but thicker, and had lumpy, sloping backs. The animals greatly resembled Earth camels except that they had six legs, three on each side—a trait all Boacan fauna seemed to share. If they had wings, Kirk mused, you'd expect them to buzz like insects, and fly away.

The animals knelt before them. Rich, embroidered saddles were draped across their backs. Clearly, they were expected to ride.

"I'm a doctor, not a rodeo cowboy," McCoy protested softly, more to himself than to anyone else, as they mounted and the creatures rose. They began to trot.

"Hang on, men. It's all in the line of duty!" Kirk called out, as he rode in front with his host, leading the party. Hand pressure on the fuzzy sides of the animals' long skinny necks seemed to regulate their speed. Spock soon rode by his side.

"These beasts are called larpas," Noro said to Kirk, and beamed. Kirk beamed back, though the bony back of the animal could be felt through the rich silk of the ruglike saddle, and the rolling of the three legs on each side being picked up and set down made for a curiously bumpy ride. The larpas called to each other in strange, comical hoots.

The historian, Rizzuto, yelled ahead to the captain. "An ancient form of transportation here, sir. The planet was pretty famous for it. Rulers still used it on state occasions until recently, and then Markor the Tyrant made old-style motor cars fashionable. Only the rulers and the very wealthy could afford those, too, but I haven't seen any . . ."

"No," Noro explained. "We in the council do not use those so much. We are hoping to soon have mechanized public transportation in big cities such as this. Such a system is already under construction on the other landmass. We thought you might like to ride larpas as, one might say, a 'traditional' welcome to Boaco Six." Again, he flashed a gap-filled smile.

People in the streets openly gawked at the passing cavalcade; children squealed and pointed.

"A royal welcome, Mr. Spock," Kirk said quietly.

"Indeed, Captain."

Some of the townspeople shouted and made disrespectful remarks. Everyone else seemed to be on foot, though some carts filled with goods were drawn by the beasts Spock had pointed out earlier, and by smaller, scrawny, miserable-looking animals. Kirk realized that riding a larpa was now a pretty exceptional way of getting around.

They're doing it because they think it will appeal to whatever romantic ideas we have about their planet. They see it as a treat. They may make speeches slandering the Federation, and officially are wary of our aid. But in their own clumsy, haphazard way, they're trying to give us the red-carpet treatment. They must, after all, want Federation support, want it very badly.

Noro gave a sharp yell, and all the larpas halted before one of the scorched and battered buildings of white stone. Cautiously, uncertainly, the landing party dismounted, McCoy moaning loudly.

Noro faced them from the middle of the stone steps, which glittered brilliantly under the glare of twin suns. "This was the palace of Puil, former ruler of the city of Boa and the lands surrounding it. We have opened it to the public as a museum, so they can see what the money that could have been bread and meat in their children's mouths was used for."

Kirk and Spock exchanged glances, and the landing party entered the palace.

They milled amongst the people of the city, let the current of people lead them. One room contained glass cells where exotic animals from all over the galaxy had been kept, in an impressive menagerie. Many of these creatures were still there, being maintained. But among these cells were the ones in which Boacan political prisoners had been kept, naked, sometimes for years, as curiosities in Puil's zoo. These cells were now empty.

Adjacent to this room was the torture room. A young man was picking up smooth metal objects from a table, explaining what each was used for to a crowd of children. The room was vast and featured an array of instruments ranging from a rack, hot pokers, and thumbscrews, to the very latest in renegade molecule rupturers and nerve center paralyzers. The young man explained that there were many subterranean chambers like this room throughout the city. "This room,

42

here in the palace, was only for Puil's very *special* guests."

McCoy, his face grim, kept a low-running commentary going on what each of the devices would do to the human body.

And then there were the ballrooms. Great round rooms festooned with dazzling candelabras; boots and bare feet moved gingerly across the floors of smoothly polished stone. Voices echoed in the stillness. The walls were a sea of mirrors; to glance around was to see oneself and those nearby duplicated hundreds of times, stretching backward into a hundred different infinities.

Courtly music could be faintly heard, like a whispering ghost of former grand parties; it came from a small section of one of the rooms which had been partitioned off. Behind the partition, old royal "home movies" of various parties and gala events were shown every hour. Kirk and his group waited to watch them from the beginning. They showed what this room had looked like in the time of Puil, filled with glittering guests and music, the images of the twirling couples flashing on the mirrored walls like bursts of color and light. The Federation men stood in the crowd and watched as the films chronicled royal festivals and party games, masques and practical jokes, pantomimes and magic acts. A poetry recital was followed by the torturing to death of a thief; both met with showers of applause and drunken delight from Puil's guests.

The coifs of the women were intricately woven and piled on their heads like jeweled mountains; the weave of the hose on the legs of the men was no less elaborate. Kirk and his friends watched the series of films through once, then moved on.

They wandered out into a maze of long, twisting staircases and corridors, encrusted with sculptures and paintings of the ruler and his family dressed in Terran Greek classical garb, in their ceremonial robes, even in Starfleet uniforms, receiving honorary decorations from the Federation. The *Enterprise* men winced at the sight. It was not pleasant to recall that the Federation had helped Puil to first achieve power.

Stemming out from the corridor were smaller ballrooms, the banquet rooms, the music chambers . . . they moved with the crowd, everyone gawking and craning their necks.

"It's fantastic. It's like some sort of grotesque amusement park," McCoy said.

"More like a treasure trove for a historian," said Rizzuto. "I hope when they get better organized they'll beef up the security and limit the number of people tracking through here. Their concept of 'giving it back' to the Boacan people is all very well, but it needs to be protected." He sighed. "How I would *love* to lose myself in research here."

"We do not know how much time we will be given to see the palace," Spock remarked, "and we may miss much of it."

"Very well, men," Kirk said. "Take advantage of this opportunity and go look at anything that interests you. We'll compare notes later."

They separated in the arch of the hallway and wandered off in different directions, freely exploring the palace with its hodgepodge of styles, more dizzying than Versailles.

Kirk followed a stream of people slipping through a hidden door in the wall of the corridor. It led to a dark tunnellike hall, and a rickety wooden stair that wound up and down through the palace—obviously a stair for servants. He followed it upward and it led to a long bare room, cramped by a low slanting ceiling, the roof of the palace. Light came in through narrow slats, hidden in the woodwork.

The people he was with stopped to listen to the account of an old man, a bent retainer from a long line of palace servants, describe what his duties had been, the hours he had worked, and what life had been like above and below stairs. His attitude seemed to change with every sentence. He was bitter about the stinginess and cruelty of Puil's family. He described the long hours, and the high rates of sickness and death among the servants matter-of-factly. Yet serving at the palace was all he had known, all he had ever been raised to dream of; his life now was without purpose. He said that the revolution had made him an antique.

The attic room was filled with a long line of narrow beds in which the servants had slept. There was a long troughlike bed stretching out at their feet; this had served as the bed for the servants' children. The dimness of the room bothered Kirk's eyes. He followed a family of Boacans out through the doorway, and down the winding staircase.

He descended all the way down to the basement level and walked out into another tunnellike corridor, past a well-stocked wine cellar, dust covering great tankards of the finest Boacan brandy. He headed on into the kitchen complex, where the stone walls seemed clammy with dank moisture. Stretching all around him was a network of stoves and carving tables, spits for roasting meat, boiling tanks and deep frying pits. New equipment that had been added in the last years of the regime augmented cruder implements, centuries old.

Old servants were on hand here as well, old chefs

and kitchen workers, to describe the work that went into the feasts they had served, the quantities of food prepared every day, for Puil's family and courtiers and for beloved pets, and the great quantities sent back uneaten. *Are they well paid by the new government to do this?* Kirk wondered. *Are they told what to say?* These servants had many harsh words for Puil. But the older chefs were openly angry at the revolution, which had deprived them of the chance to practice and profit from their art; the common people could not afford it, and the new rulers refused their services.

There were small bedrooms down here as well, filled with berths for the kitchen staff. There were great chimney flues, and the visiting Boacan children crawled inside them to look around and emerged covered with soot. Children had been used, in Puil's day, for the cleaning of chimneys, and other such specialized work. Kirk knew if he lingered down here too long, he would have to leave much of the rest of the palace unexplored.

Stepping from the twilight of the servants' stairway out into the main hall of a higher floor caused Kirk to blink several times, from the brightness of the light. Light was the thing most revered on Boaco Six, and a well-lit home thus a sign of prestige. The palace was illuminated by vast windows of crystal and stained glass, aided by some artificial sources. Once his eyes adjusted, Kirk became aware of space-age noises which seemed incongruous in such a place, on such a world.

He walked along and discovered a laser room with a built-in light show unit, and a children's arcade—all the equipment was an example of modern state of the art Federation technology. Children visiting the

46

palace-museum were allowed to play laser battles in the arcade. They whooped as they aimed and blasted at each other's targets. Such expensive, sophisticated equipment seemed unreal on a backwater world such as this.

In another wing, Kirk found a succession of sumptuous bedrooms and boudoirs, closets stuffed with clothes, wardrobes and vanities dripping with jewelry. It was a banquet of opulence, spread out for inspection. Women wandered, murmured, reached out their fingers to stroke a plush or glittering object—and then drew back their hands, afraid. A guilty atmosphere seemed to hang over the people here, as if they were raiders, trespassers in a temple. This mood affected the children less; they caught up and exclaimed over shiny trinkets, and ran their feet back and forth in the layers of deep downy carpeting.

Kirk encountered young Ensign Michaels in a room filled with women's stockings, girdles, and other undergarments. The stockings were piled high on the bed in a rainbow of colors, a dozen of every pair, and a mountain of satiny drawers was spilling off a reclining couch. A portrait of one of Puil's fat mistresses hung over the vanity in a gilded frame. She was dressed as a Terran shepherdess, and coquettishly held a jeweled shepherd's crook. A small, fuzzy, six-legged animal, with an orange bow around its throat, rubbed its head against her dress. The portrait was illuminated by a large lamp built into the wall above it, and it was at this fluorescent source of light that the Boacans gazed with wonder. Candlelight was still the reality in their homes.

Michaels stared around him, his face expressing awe and nausea. It was what his captain felt as well.

Chapter Five

THE SEA OF STARS is supposed to be unchanging. For the ocean mariner or the star traveler, these points of light are the constant in the abyss. Their pattern, seen from different latitudes, is a coded message to set his compass with, and steer by. The light of a sun at the other side of the galaxy, that may have long since exploded or quietly died, reaches across the light-years, and its steady beam is as reassuring as an anchor in the vacuum of darkness.

And yet, the impossible seemed to be happening. Readings had been blinking and shifting for several days. Pockets of stars seemed to invert their constellations, as if to suggest that the quadrant had been crossed, and they were being viewed from the opposite angle. Clusters of asteroid debris had been appearing and disappearing, clusters not on any Federation star map. Their formation wasn't like anything you'd find in a meteor shower. All this spelled only one thing: sensor readings foul-up.

It had to be the fault of this shoddy company

equipment. Ion storms were making the sensors go on the fritz and report screwy things. They'd be fine for hours, readings would be normal, and then they'd pull one of these maneuvers. It was irritating, unnerving, even, but it didn't add up to a major problem. The ship could navigate around these asteroids, real or imagined. Close to any object, safety systems would come into play and steer clear of collision. But the entire system would need an overhaul when it docked.

Glen Andrews swiveled around on his chair and stretched his legs out in front of him. They ached from lack of use. God, was he restless—he felt ready to scream. Boredom stultified his mind, and he felt that if he tried one more time to get to the source of these blips in the sensor readings, he'd bug out completely.

At one time, navigating an ore freighter from a mineral-laden planet to a young Federation colony had seemed a cushy, relaxing, well-paying job— exciting, even. Just the thing for a young man ready to cut loose from Earth, anxious to see the galaxy, with a hatred of punching time clocks, and the business grind. Just the way to get needed experience, and stories to swap, and to meet exotic girls . . .

After three years of such work, it seemed like a penal sentence. He was uncertain about when he'd have the courage to set himself free.

Some adventure, he thought. *Interstellar navigation. Big deal. When your ship just plods along through space at warp two. When the freight you're hauling isn't very valuable, or even explosive. About as exciting and glamorous as navigating a garbage scow. Just once, I'd like to see a little action.*

He spun around on the chair once more, and stopped it to lean forward and grimly observe his only shipmate and companion, Hiroshi Takehara. Hiroshi was absorbed in using gravity beams to make a small metal ball go through a hoop inside a fiberglass box. His brow creased with concentration as he shifted the gravity levers up and down.

Amazing what three months of this tedious traveling will drive a man to, thought Glen.

"Hey, Hiroshi. I've got another exciting game you could try. You stand and bang your head against the wall and see which cracks first."

"Be quiet, man! I've almost got it." Hiroshi licked his lips and subtly adjusted the right-hand lever. "Banzai!"

Glen got up and sauntered over to him to take note of his achievement, but he shook his head as he went. "I don't know, Takehara. I'm worried about you. I think you need some time in a rest colony, weaving basket lanterns and polishing glo-rocks."

"Aah, you're just jealous." Hiroshi put the toy aside and moved toward the control panel his friend had abandoned. "You couldn't do it if you tried."

"Hey, do you see me trying?" Glen pressed a button on the wall food dispenser, in hope of a glass of beer. But the machine flashed a refusal—he had had a glass an hour ago, and the alcohol intake of freighter pilots was regulated. He punched the bulkhead and swore. "I'm cracking up. I swear to God, I really am. Look, distract me, get my mind off being cooped up in this tin can. Tell me about whatever was on that news service wire you were picking up, before the storm struck."

"You can't assume it's an ion storm. In fact, I'm really worried, Glen . . ."

"All right, fine. Then, before the equipment started

being more useless than usual. Just gimme the headline stories, please."

"Glen, Glen," Hiroshi said, shaking his head in a way calculated to irritate his friend. "Why don't you ever read about these things for yourself?"

"Hey, did I know communications were going to go kablooey? Anyhow, maybe I want *your* expert interpretation of current events. What did it say about peace talks? Or war talks?"

Hiroshi's face became more serious. "Same as it's been. Nothing erupting yet, but the situation doesn't look good. The Romulans want to renegotiate the borders of their neutral zone—but they're really just using that as a pretext, they seem to be gunning for some kind of war. Some 'anonymous' Federation Council aide thinks they're worried by rumors that Starfleet has some new ship or system up its sleeve. They don't want to just sit around waiting for our side to deploy it."

Glen really, really wanted that beer. He could imagine its cold, bitter wetness sliding down his throat. "And the Klingons?"

"The Klingons are pretty gung ho also. They say this situation is just typical of Federation thinking—that we think we can just divide up and demarcate the galaxy, draw lines around everybody else. They're worried the Romulans are being mistreated." As he talked, Hiroshi kept his eye on the control panel Glen had moved away from. He had had some training in engineering, and he found the occasional distortion of readings more bizarre than did his friend. But all looked quiet now, just as it should be.

Glen was amused by the Klingon stand. *"They're* worried about the Romulans? That's a laugh and a half. You know that something is up when the Klingons start playing good Samaritan."

A chief difficulty, every day Glen logged in space, was trying to find ways to look busy. Not that Hiroshi needed to be impressed, or anything. But Hiroshi seemed to have a much clearer idea of where his duties began and ended; he'd execute them precisely, then relax in reading or contemplation. Or with his blasted gravity box.

Whereas Glen always felt a need to prove himself, prove that his job had meaning, his presence was necessary. That he couldn't, after all, be conveniently replaced by a mechanical iron ore freighter. He paced about now, and paused to run his hands over a series of wall circuits, checking for—what? Dust? Short-circuited fuses?

"All right, then, what were the other big stories? Tell me about this 'miracle man' you were saying lives in this quadrant."

Hiroshi yawned. "Didn't I tell you about him, already?"

"Yeah, you were jabbering about it this morning. But since when do I pay attention to what you say? Tell me again, what's all the fuss about him for?"

"Well," Hiroshi said, "it's this guy called Flint. The bulletin came in at 2200 hours, when you were sacked out. The Federation has confirmed that he's everyone he says he is."

"So, who does he say he is?"

"Everyone, practically. Methuselah, Merlin, Solomon . . ."

"Who?"

"Great men, Andrews, great men. And from *your* Western cultural heritage. Shame on you for not knowing about them."

"So the idea is, this guy is incredibly old, and *that's* how he was able to be all these people?" Glen's hands stopped their idle run over the exposed circuits. He leaned back against the wall, taken with the idea.

"That's what they say. And now he's doing some 'weapons research' for Starfleet." Hiroshi smiled slyly. "And if you really want *my* opinion," he added, "I'll bet this has something to do with whatever has got the Romulans so worried."

"Uh-huh. What kind of weapons research?"

"Come on, Andrews. It's classified. Top secret. You know, the big time."

Glen Andrews scratched his ear. He felt almost miffed at not being told, not having his drowsy curiosity satisfied. "And you expect me to believe all this stuff? A load of bunk you read off some cheesy star tabloid news wire, about a mystery man who lives forever?"

"The bulletin came on the Starfleet news wire service," Hiroshi said evenly. "I'd hardly call them a 'cheesy star tabloid' operation."

Glen knew he could not really challenge this. "You know," he finally drawled, "I once thought about joining Starfleet."

"You? What a joke."

"But I couldn't handle the haircut. Or the uniform."

"Or the regular baths," Hiroshi gibed. "I hear they require those too."

"Yeah . . . that's the way to see the galaxy," his friend said, not really hearing him. "But I guess, with things heating up like they are, it wouldn't be a very smart time to try and enlist." This thought ended his Starfleet dreaming. "Okay, Hiroshi. If this guy Flint is

53

in the neighborhood, why don't we pay a visit to his planet?"

"Are you kidding me? Uh-uh. He's got his own private world. Think how rich he must be! Admirers, the press, and dignitaries have tried to get through to him. But he's put up a force-field, to keep 'em out. I mean, he's in contact with Starfleet and all. I think it was a starship that first stumbled across him and identified him. Anyhow, he's in this quadrant all right, but nowhere near us."

"And as long as we're crawling along in this snail of a ship, we'd be older than he is by the time we got there. And the company would give us hell, of course. God, am I getting stir-crazy."

"You really need to relax."

"I'll tell you what we both need, Hiroshi. A couple of weeks on some pleasure planet. Or at a starbase, say Starbase Twelve. They've got this one little café there, Xandar's it's called . . ."

"I've told you what we ought to do, Glen. We need to get out of this line of work altogether." Hiroshi checked the ship's life-support readings, speed, and fuel consumption. Sensors showed that no other ships were in the area. He would let the ship's remote control navigate, for a while longer. "What we really need to do is open a place of our own . . ."

"Aw, not this again!"

"Say on Gallaga Nine. A lot of freighters pass through that system, and the clubs are generally lousy. But after a year in this line, *we* know what needs guys have when they're resting up. Not sleazy, noisy stop-overs, but a place that's classy, relaxing. Fine liqueurs, dimmed lights, soft music, a fountain, maybe. And we could rent out rooms . . ."

"Aw, listen, Hiroshi. I've been an ore puller for

three years, not one. And I know what guys *really* want after a month of hauling a load through space. And it ain't soft music and cherry blossom wine. Have you been to this place Xandar's? Have you?"

"I really don't want to . . ."

"It's the only jumping joint on Starbase Twelve. Hell, you should see the girls they have. They have one girl, a green Orion, well, you know what *they're* like. In her first number, she comes out in this getup, it looks like jade green swaying fronds. And she's even got jade green tassles on her . . ."

"I get the idea." Now it was Hiroshi's turn to amble across the room and take a stab at the food dispenser panel. He punched a few buttons and wrinkled his nose in distaste when the reconstituted string bean tempura arrived on his tray.

"As I was saying," Glen continued, unperturbed, "a couple of swigs of Saurian brandy, and this girl will transport you to green heaven. And then there's Sadie . . ."

Both men heard it at the same moment. Both snapped their heads around to listen. It was a high-pitched whine, almost like a woman shrieking. Their lazed, long-numbed minds identified it after a few moments—someone had fired a phaser blast, and the shot had grazed their ship.

Hiroshi dropped his food tray and ran to the control panel. "My God, we're being attacked! But by whom? Where did they come from?"

Glen moved beside him, activated the main viewer. A small craft seemed to shimmer in space for an instant, then winked away into nothing. Sensors could only pick up readings of scattered asteroid rubble.

"What . . . it looked like a Federation make . . ." Glen puzzled.

The ship reappeared, as Hiroshi switched on the ore freighter's flimsy shields. Immediately after, the attacking vessel fired another shot, damaging the shields, and sending shock waves through their ship.

Glen crouched to repair a wire grill that clattered open, the inner wires it protected heating and hissing. "Oh God, oh my God, oh God, help me, oh God . . ."

"They vanished again. What the hell is this?"

"Hiroshi, contact them. Hail them, and tell them we give up. They want the goddamn iron ore so badly, they can have it."

"No, Glen, we can't. We must defend . . ."

"Defend? Defend how? With what?" Glen stood, his face red with hysteria. "Is our ship armed? Has the company given us any means of protecting ourselves?"

"Well, who would attack an ore freighter?"

"Well, if these . . . space pirates want our cargo so badly, they're gonna come take it anyway. Tell them we surrender."

Hiroshi set his jaw, determined not to comply. A second later, another phaser beam blasted through their shields, and the ship began to creak and fold in places, like tin being crumpled. Hiroshi dived for the intercom. "We surrender, we surrender. Help! Stop it, please, stop it!"

Only static came filtering back, filling their now-darkened cabin. And then a maniacal laugh.

"Please," Hiroshi whispered.

The next phaser blast ripped away the cargo carrier so that it floated off into space. Equipment flew through the small pilot's chamber, and the life-support monitor began to blink. Glen Andrews found himself lying in the darkness, wedged under part of the control panel, which had ripped itself out of the wall. His head throbbed. He felt a warm trickle of blood from his scalp, seeping through his hair, curling behind his ear, and forming a puddle under his head. His collar was sticky. The room was dark, and very quiet. His right leg was numb.

"Hiroshi?" he called. There was no response. He shut his eyes and tried to brace himself for the inevitable final phaser blast, to finish them off. It did not come. Instead, amid the crackling static, several voices could be heard.

"Jahn?"

"Did you see it? They never even touched me! Did you see it, I got them, I scored a perfect hit, as easy as bouncing a bird with a stone!"

"No, Jahn, please, come away from there. My God, what have you done . . ." Sobs followed.

"But they're Grups, Rhea. Now they've been neutralized. They can't tell the others where we are. I blitzed them, I beat them, I pulverized them, I won . . ." The male voice trailed off too, into feebleness and uncertainty.

Glen Andrews felt a sick and dizzy distance from the talking that reminded him of a puppet show. Now the girl spoke again. "Let go, Jahn, let me have that, please. Here, see, look where we're heading . . ."

The crackling voices died away.

Chapter Six

AFTER SEVERAL HOURS in the palace-turned-museum in the city of Boa, each member of the *Enterprise* landing party was sought out by a messenger from Noro, the minister of education, and told that it was time to leave. They met again on the palace steps. Morning had given way to a brilliant afternoon, which dazzled as brightly as the palace had. The heat was oppressive.

"Well, Captain," Spock said, "I for one feel I've explored the palace thoroughly."

"I think we all got a sense of the place," Kirk agreed, "and I see no need for individual reports."

They rode back to the public square on the bony backs of the larpas, guiding the beasts absently, their minds filled with images of Puil's excesses, their heads bent in somber silence. Noro sensed their mood and made no attempt to chat or moralize on the lessons of the museum.

Around them, the city hummed with life. Many women had set up large weaving looms in front of their houses; they pulled their shuttles back and forth, slipping them through the course threads with firm strokes, leaving in their wake intricate patterns in a richly textured cloth. They called out to their friends, seated by looms in front of the houses next to them and opposite, swapped stories and jokes. Children tugged at the hems of their thick skirts and were given bits of string to play with. Older girls were made to sit very still nearby and watch, or select a color, or occasionally to push the shuttle through the loom, calloused older hands over their own, guiding them.

The rich, dizzying fabric of the women's skirts and blouses showed themselves to be the product of such looms. The diagonal slant of the loom cloth hung on the wooden frame created a kind of triangular tent. In the shade underneath, babies slept, peacefully shielded from bugs and the heat, their mothers' toes nearby, to lend reassurance.

Once the landing party reached the public square and dismounted, they were introduced to new ministers and program heads, and each member was escorted by one of these worthies to view a different aspect of the city.

Noro himself approached McCoy. "It has fallen to me to escort you, Doctor. I realize you found the larpa ride difficult. And so I have arranged a means of transport I hope will be more comfortable."

He led the way up the road to where an old-style motor car, something on the order of a Model-T Ford, McCoy guessed, was standing. They got in, Noro started the vehicle with difficulty, and the machine headed off in the direction of the forest. *Or is it based on some other make of old-style automobile?* McCoy wondered to himself. *Sulu, if he were here, would know the year, model, and make—to me it just looks like a big, noisy box.* Too relieved to ponder the issue further, McCoy sank back into the cushioned seat.

As they drove, Noro spoke to him of the literacy campaign, his proudest pet project. Those precious few inhabitants of Boaco Six who had received an education, or at least had acquired the skill of reading, were being given small government subsidies to pass the gift on to their families and villages; teams were being sent out to reach people in remote areas. Soon the funds allotted by the Council of Youngers for this project would run dry; Noro and his ministry would then have to rely on volunteers to carry on the work. The heady goal they had set for themselves was to have a literate planet within the space of three years.

They followed the road leading out of the city that the *Enterprise* men had beamed so far from the night before. Their car was the only vehicle, and they the only travelers braving the midday heat. Twenty miles out, Noro slowed the bulky motor vehicle to a halt. A dismal looking air-skimmer was parked nearby, crushing the grasses beneath it and sinking its gliders into the mud. Again, McCoy was no engineer, but it looked to him like a piece of mechanical junk, styled for a gullible primitive market. Noro shot him an apologetic look, and they climbed in through the narrow hatchway.

They seated themselves in its cylindrical chamber which, McCoy noted, lacked several important safety features. Noro pushed a few buttons, turned a few knobs, and the thing staggered into the air. The seat was too hard, the ride much too bumpy. The machine trembled and vibrated as if afraid of flight, as if conscious of its own ineptitude. McCoy could feel again pangs of protest in his backside, as he had during the larpa ride—sharp reminders of why he preferred life Earthside, or aboard the *Enterprise,* to "roughing it."

Noro saw him trying to grin and bear it. "I must apologize, Doctor, for this vehicle. Not very smooth sailing, I'm afraid."

"Well, maybe that'll teach you, next time, not to buy Klingon-made hardware." McCoy's tone was gruff and belligerent.

"We are of your mind, Doctor, many of us," Noro said. "But truly, given the current attitude of your manufacturers, and the Federation embargo on trade with our people—do we have much choice?"

McCoy had no reply to that. The gliders of the air-skimmer dipped and dragged in the branches and leaves of the trees and vines they were flying over, sending birds and chattering animals flurrying in all directions. McCoy wondered how long it would be before one of the purple vine tendrils wrapped itself around a glider and would not let go, and the air-skimmer came crashing down in a sputtering circle. *Some air-skimmer. Air-bludgeoner is more like it.* A double dose of sunlight poured through the glass dome, magnified by its curve; the glare was almost unbearable.

At last the rumbling machine began its short descent, and touched down, with a jolt, in a jungle clearing. Two tall trees stood at the center of the clearing. A roof of thatch was built around their trunks, beams lashed on, and covered with foliage. It made for a circular shelter, and a coarse tarpaulin was tacked onto the edges of the roof, and spilled down over the sides to form walls.

A line of children and adults wound out from under this canvas. The people waited patiently, though some looked frightened. The children were more subdued here than in the city, some crying and burying their heads in their mothers' skirts, some playing quietly in the tall grass.

"Our health drive to reach people in remote areas on this landmass was begun last month," Noro said. "This modest clinic is the nerve center for that effort, in this region. Our doctors and family health teachers go out from this point, and they report back here, every week."

He called out to the person in charge of the clinic. No one appeared. He called again.

While they waited, McCoy noticed three people by the edge of the forest, talking, two men and a young woman. One of the men did not look Boacan, and the woman obviously was not. The jumpsuit she wore was of fashionable mauve. Its folds flashed elegance as she moved. Her boots were high-heeled, delicate, and impractical for such marshy terrain. A belt of crystal loops cinched her suit and showed off her shapely waist. Her long blond hair showered down her back and resolved itself in a braid at the bottom.

Noro took in McCoy's puzzled glance. "They are Federation tourists," he explained, "who asked to be shown various sites. That Boacan man with them is their guide. Perhaps you will get to meet them later."

"Tourists?" McCoy asked, incredulous. "The Federation has issued strong 'recommendations,' or 'warnings,' or whatever you want to call them, telling civilians to avoid this world."

"Nevertheless, some people from your Federated Planets have been willing to brave our hospitality. Especially humans and Vulcans. Many volunteers have been helpful to us in construction work and farming, and two of the best doctors operating out of this clinic are from your planet Earth."

McCoy pondered this, another fact not discussed in Starfleet reports, another wrinkle in the balance of power game.

"We still get our share of missionaries, of course," Noro continued with a smile, "from various sects. Those visitors we could easily do without. We discourage them from staying long, and our people are not very receptive to their efforts."

"And these people?" McCoy said, pointing.

Noro hesitated a moment before replying, searching for a tactful response. "They are, perhaps, typical of another type of visitor to Boaco Six. Very well meaning. But I believe, for them, defying your Federation's advice about coming here is something of a game. A 'safari' into adventure, or rebelliousness."

"Mmm, well, bored rich kids need their amusements, I suppose," McCoy said.

Noro called out again to the person in charge, and at last she appeared, lifting up a corner of the canvas tarpaulin, rising up from under it. She straightened and rolled down her sleeves. "No more tours of the clinic," she said crossly, "we are very busy today—" Then she had a good look at them. Her expression softened as she approached them.

"I'm a Starfleet doctor, ma'am," McCoy said, "and I can appreciate that you're busy. But I'd like to see the inside of your clinic, if you don't mind, and maybe I can help out around here. At least, for today."

"Of course, Doctor," the young Boacan woman said. "We were told you might be coming." She put out her hand, and McCoy grasped it. "My name is Ona, and I'm running the clinic for this rotation."

"Our minister of health is on the other landmass at present," Noro explained, "but Ona will show you around. I shall return here and bring you back to the

63

city of Boa, in five hours' time. Good-bye." He headed for the air-skimmer, then turned and offered his gapped smile once again. "And I will look for a cushion for your seat, Doctor." Then he left.

McCoy forgot all thoughts of his own discomfort as Ona lifted the edge of the canvas from the wet grass, and they both ducked under it. Inside the clinic there were more waiting people, on thin wooden benches and on the ground. Health workers moved rapidly within a cluttered thirty-foot area, asking questions and attending to needs.

"This clinic is part of a much larger program," Ona told McCoy. "Our 'Hospital Without Walls' program. The idea is, our doctors make their rounds to see families and workers living in the jungle, checking in on those with critical illnesses as regularly as they would on ward patients in a typical hospital. Or at least, that's a goal we're shooting for."

"And the people here?"

"Have new problems, or emergencies. Or are coming to tell us where they live. Or for advice."

Their discussion was stopped, as they watched a boy of fifteen on Ona's staff take a boy of seven from the arms of his mother. As the woman described her son's symptoms, the health worker nodded.

"He's suffering from severe dehydration," he told her. "I'll prepare a saline solution."

The woman asked about the solution, and then wanted to know if the salt water of the ocean would not do just as well. She and her family lived not far from the coast, and her son had been sick this way before.

Ona stepped in to answer her firmly. "No, it would *not* do just as well. If you gave your son seawater in an attempt to treat this, you would jeopardize his life. We

64

will send someone to your house tomorrow, to check and see if you need more saline."

As the boy was being treated, she turned back to McCoy. "And that is one of our greatest challenges— educating people. We hope, after our people in the field have had a chance to teach families the basics of disease prevention and sanitary living, and some do-it-yourself remedies, clinics like this one will be less crowded."

"People here are unfamiliar with the basic rules of hygiene?"

"People this far from the city are. And there are women here," Ona said tightly, "who used to buy food packets from Federation manufacturers that claimed that their synthetic foodstuffs would be better for children than a natural diet. Made some pretty impossible claims for themselves."

"Companies like that are considered irresponsible by everyone," McCoy told her earnestly. "They are censored by the medical community and by the public."

"I'm sure they are. At any rate, these women would buy up these packets, feed their children the dangerous powders and capsules, until they could not afford more. So they'd water them down, or feed the children sporadically. Children and mothers, you see, developed a phobia of real food."

Ona picked up a tray, filled with clotted blood, and briskly began to scrub it with a wire brush in a wooden tub full of black Boacan water. "We lost many, many children in this way. But those companies do not come here anymore. That, at least, is one positive side effect of the Federation trade embargo."

McCoy watched the treatment and dispatch of patients, occasionally offering his arms to hold a baby, or a word of advice. From Ona's speech pattern and manner, he guessed she had received her medical training at a Federation school, before the revolution. There was no chance to talk to her about her past, however, as she wound bandages, cauterized a wound, treated a burn patient for shock.

The shiny black water used to clean cuts and sores made McCoy feel queasy and anxious; he mentally shouted to himself that it was clean, sterile, perfectly safe.

The clinic was understaffed, and woefully lacking in facilities and medicine. In many cases, cleansing and painkillers were all that could be offered. But McCoy could see that their education program was already beginning to be effective. A family brought in a man strapped down to a body-board. The family income came from robbing nests of precious eggs, and he had had a fall from a high tree. He would have to be treated in the city of Boa, would travel back in the air-skimmer with Noro and McCoy.

McCoy winced at the thought of a victim of such injuries enduring the bumpy ride. Neural damage to the spine was probable. McCoy took his medical scanner from its kit, and as it gently whirred near the man's neck, the reading confirmed these fears.

While Ona praised the family for the way they had used the body-board, McCoy wrestled with himself. All the patients being brought in here, all the people lined up outside, could be treated so much more quickly and effectively aboard the *Enterprise*. Why, he alone, if he had the proper medical equipment and drugs beamed down, could do so much . . .

You're here as an observer. You're here to see how effective they are, he reminded himself. It was the same dilemma he faced when he saw inadequate health facilities on any primitive world. And yet, the Prime Directive . . .

A small girl was brought in with rabies. Ona's face showed the distress she felt upon seeing the girl, with foam clinging to her lips, though it was obviously not the first case the clinic had dealt with.

"I thought you had some kind of vaccine program against this," McCoy said.

Ona turned sharply. "We do. But it is impossible to reach everyone, impossible. In the time of Markor and Puil, many families fled to the mountains, the forests, the jungles, to live in isolation, beyond the reach of the rulers. Their customs revolve around hiding now, they distrust all governments, including the new revolutionary one. How are we, Doctor, with no resources, to find people who don't want to be found?"

Pain was in her voice. She took the girl's chin gently in her hand and turned the small head to examine the bite on the cheek. The girl whimpered that the bite felt strange now, that it tingled.

Her grandmother told the story. The girl h. d been bitten twenty days before by a small feral jungle animal, a wooker.

Jim was lucky to get away from that animal that attacked him without a bite or scratch. Damned lucky.

The child had seemed fine until a few days ago. Then her forehead became hot, she complained of feeling dizzy. Her mother had offered her soup that contained traditional healing herbs, thinking it might help. The girl raised a cup of the soup to her lips. Then she began to convulse. Soup came spitting out of her mouth, her neck tightened, she took hours to calm.

Now she was terrified of all liquids, had had none for days, and even a draft of wind made her grab her throat and scream that she was suffocating.

Ona shook her head. "Hydrophobia. When the furious rabies are this far along, there is nothing we can do. There are some drugs in the city that will prolong the child's life a little, but we are talking of a matter of days."

The girl gave no indication of having heard or understood. Her maroon eyes were glazed, her pupils dilated, and she groped for her grandmother's hand.

"I can give you painkillers," Ona continued in a hollow voice, "and tranquilizers for when her condition worsens. My assistant will explain to you how to keep the rest of the family safe from catching it." She added, very softly, "You see, she might become violent, might bite, or scratch."

McCoy's internal battle became more fierce. *The Prime Directive? What does it matter, what can it mean here? We waived it when it came to transporters and phasers. Our orders said not to give them new technology—but command meant just weaponry. The Federation has not classed this as a contamination-free developing culture.*

He knew that this planet had been visited by humans long before the Prime Directive was formulated and passed by the Federation. Every person on Boaco Six knew that there were other cultures, other worlds more advanced than their own. Federation advisers had served Puil, the planet had not been shielded. The disease of rabies itself was an early, unasked-for, gift from Earth, in the days when restrictions on the interplanetary transportation of animals were not enforced. And he had read how widespread the rabies problem on Boaco Six had become.

The struggle within him was resolved. He turned to Ona. "This child isn't going to die. We have drugs aboard the *Enterprise* that can save her, even this late in the game. And that man"—he indicated the figure strapped to the body-board—"isn't going to be transported anywhere." He took a deep breath. "Unless it's up to our ship."

The lines on Ona's face began to relax. Doctors on some planets felt offended at having their local practices superseded, but she, as a Federation trainee, realized he was offering the best help available. "An embargo on caring is thus temporarily lifted," she said quietly. "Thank you, Doctor."

The grandmother, who had doubled over keening, was helped up by an assistant, and she now asked what was going on. McCoy flicked open his communicator and asked that a medical team stand by in the transporter room for patients, and that Christine Chapel gather together a number of serums and beam down to assist him at the clinic.

"I know it's irregular, Lieutenant," he said to the guard on transporter duty, "and I don't care. Get on it right away."

Chapter Seven

AFTER THE EMERGENCY PATIENTS were beamed up to the ship, McCoy walked outside the clinic, in the shade of the giant trees supporting its roof. He knew it would be some time before Nurse Chapel had all the drugs he required and had processed some not in storage. There were some diseases, endemic to this planet, that his medical scanner had never encountered before; for the people with these he could do nothing. But everyone at that clinic who could be helped would be.

It's a gamble whether Starfleet will approve of this. We are still at odds with the government here. But morally, it's no gamble. It's the only thing I can do. And, in case it's bending the rules more than it seems, I want to be the one responsible. I don't want Jim's neck on the line for this.

At the end of the queue snaking out from the clinic, talking to the people who waited, McCoy again saw the Federation tourists. The young lady was trying to get a laugh out of a miserable-looking child; the child was not responding.

McCoy ambled over. She became aware of his presence, took in his uniform, and glared.

"What are you doing here? Haven't you done enough to these people? How many of you are there? Does the Council of Youngers know you're here?"

"Oh, there are a few more of us down here. And the council is taking real good care of us." McCoy let his geniality lightly mock her abrasiveness. "They wanted me to see this facility. Now, how 'bout you? What brings you to Boaco Six?"

The blond girl's little nose twitched. "Indignation. Outrage. Disgust. It's totally unbelievable what the Federation is doing to these people, so I'm here to lend support."

"Where? In farming, house building, maybe . . ."

"No," she snapped. "Moral support. We're here on an outreach tour. My husband and me."

The man had appeared out of the crowd and was now hovering by her protectively. Their Boacan guide stood a short distance away.

"Why are the Boacans providing you with this tour?" McCoy asked.

"Is this some kind of Starfleet interrogation?" the girl asked defiantly, perhaps hopefully. "Are you trying to crack down on people like us?"

McCoy shook his head. "Nope. That probably wouldn't be worth the effort. It was just out of curiousity that I asked."

"Well, they're showing us around because I guess they think it's time the galaxy learned the truth and someone exposed the way you're persecuting and dominating these people."

"Persecuting how?"

"Well, with the embargo and . . . stuff."

71

"Ah." *She hasn't done her homework,* McCoy mused. *Even I could lambaste us better than that.*

"And plus, I guess they're glad to show us around because we paid for the tour. That's another way we're helping. We paid the highest rate, so we got the full works. My husband's going to get to keep a genuine rifle, used by one of the council members. And they taught us some of their songs and cheers. And we get to visit practically *everywhere.*"

Warming to her subject, she seemed to forget for the moment that McCoy, as a Starfleet officer, was evil incarnate. "And I was in the market all day yesterday. It was *so* colorful, *so* wild. I took some of the most amazing projections of the native people. They are *so* colorful, *so* great."

"You brought your projection cube with you?"

"Well, of course. Here, let me show you my best one. I took it of this little girl I saw selling vegetables."

She reached into a silken pouch attached to the crystal belt at her waist. Her long, manicured fingers drew out the black cube and fumbled with the mechanism.

"It was funny. I wanted her to pose for me, but she wouldn't. She said she'd seen a projection once before, and she thought I would be stealing her soul, or capturing it in my 'box,' or something really bizarre. Finally, her brothers and sisters got her to do it. But not until after I'd given them over a hundred credits worth of—I've got it!"

She flicked the switch, and a glowing projection shot out of the cube and shimmered in the air before them. Within its three-dimensional matrix, the image of a scared-looking little girl took form, skinny, in a cotton shift. Fresh green and black and maroon produce were arrayed behind her. McCoy knew that an intelligent computer, if fed this projection, would be able to touch it up, perhaps give the little girl a cuter, happier expression.

"Isn't she beautiful?" the projectionist murmured. "When I get home, I'm going to have it filled out, so it looks solid, and projected permanently on our lawn."

Where *was* her home? Judging from the cut of the luxurious jumpsuit, the Martian colony, McCoy guessed. This girl seemed to be of that "type." He imagined the filled-in form of this little Boacan child standing on a synthetic lawn under the grand colony atmosphere dome, the house arching up behind, as a backdrop. And this would be . . . something on the order of a lawn ornament? A garden gnome?

"How much longer is your tour going to be?" he asked.

"We're extending it," she said, switching off the projection cube with a click, and slipping it into the silk bag. "But I'll tell you, we're not seeing everything we're supposed to. Like that woman in there"—she pointed toward the clinic tent—"is not cooperating *at all*. She let us in there for hardly five minutes. And after we flew out here, to this nowhere, in one of those horrible machines!"

McCoy sympathized with her indignation. If roughing it didn't agree with him, how hard must it be on this poor princess?

"And you should see the place they're putting us up in Boa," she continued. "Insects on the walls sometimes. And they give us all this bizarre spicy alien food. But it's worth it to, um, absorb the primitive atmosphere."

McCoy saw the Boacan guide's mouth twitch. With amusement?

The doctor pulled at his ear. "Pretty inconsiderate of them, though, sending you way out here, where you might get that nice outfit messed up."

The girl stared at him. She was remembering again that he was the enemy, and became furious. "You think this is some kind of joke, don't you? Yeah, you can be all condescending to me, you can treat people who want to help your victims like they don't matter, but let me tell you, *sir*—"

"Easy, honey," her husband said, touching her shoulder, but she shrugged his hand away, and the blond mane shook behind her.

"I'm proud to support the Boacan Revolution, and I feel like I'm half-Boacan already, and in case you're wondering, my father is a very important, highly influential . . ."

McCoy tuned her out. These people weren't even worth baiting. Yet there was something that *was* important, something he should ask them about, that was not so trivial. What was it?

A whirring filled the air, and Nurse Chapel shimmered into being a few feet away from them in the clearing. As she materialized, the Boacans waiting on line gasped and pointed. A small boy ran forward to touch her, then ran back to the line and dove behind his mother. Chapel carried a large, opaque medicine kit, the vials and hypos glinting in the sunlight. The sight of them jogged McCoy's memory.

"Your reinforcements?" the girl sneered.

"Yes. Yes, and that reminds me. Were y'all properly immunized before you came to this world?"

"Immunized against what?"

"The native diseases. Here you are, hanging around a health clinic. Are you protected?"

"That's *our* concern, thanks. If this is some kind of ploy to scare us, it's not going to—"

"You'd better let me give you both vaccines for the most common Boacan diseases," McCoy said calmly. "Matter of fact, you're *going* to let me."

Nurse Chapel, hearing the exchange, called up to the *Enterprise* and ordered that several more hypos be beamed down.

"Do you think we're going to submit to this?" the girl demanded. "Do you think we can be ordered to—"

"Honey, be reasonable," her husband said. He turned to McCoy. "Yeah, it's probably a good idea that we get the shots. Thanks."

His wife pouted, then finally agreed.

Ensign Michaels was not escorted by any Boacan minister to have a program explained or to view a project in progress. The captain gave him leave, instead, to wander the city of Boa and get to know its people.

"Talk to people," Kirk urged, "but most of all, let them do the talking. Don't jump on them, coax them out; just sit back and observe."

"Yes, sir," Michaels said stiffly.

"And for heaven's sake, Ensign, don't say anything too inflammatory. The last thing we could afford now is some kind of diplomatic incident. I'm counting on you, Michaels," he said with a smile, to soften the implied reproach.

"Yes, sir!" Michaels cried again.

At ease, Kirk thought, then wondered if the boy knew the meaning of those words.

Michaels left the public square and wandered down

a dusty, winding back street, viewing it with suspicion, nearly jumping in the air when a low-crawling mangy animal, dragging along a pouch full of babies in the dust, batted him with its snout.

He drew a few curious glances, and a few laughing propositions from the weaving women seated along the roadside, which caused him to hurry on.

At the end of the road an old gutted building half stood, the stone of its walls crumbling, the wooden beams of its roof crashing down to form a triangular sheltering darkness. Michaels's heart began to pound. As he determined to explore the ruin, his mind filled with undefined, lightning thoughts of secret meetings and cults, espionage or counterespionage, heroes or rogues who might be hiding there. He bent his head and entered.

His eyes took a while to grow accustomed to the dark. Part of a wall blocked his way, he saw, but beyond it there *was* a light, and some kind of activity. He inched his way along. A beam above him snapped, he looked up, and then an agile force tackled him, and brought him crashing to the ground. White terror gripped Michaels, a tension in his chest telling him that this was not a game, that he was out of his depth, that he should never have left home . . .

His shoulders were pinioned down into the rubble and dust. He opened his eyes and saw above him the laughing face of a boy his age. The boy seemed to enjoy his fear; the face was mocking, but not cruel.

"Look at you," the stranger said. "Here I expected some troublemaker from a rival gang, and I land on a little spaceman. I think someone is *very* lost." He eased off and allowed Michaels to get up and dust himself off. Michaels glared, but could not stop shaking.

"I'm not lost. I'm here to observe your planet," he said. "You didn't have to attack me."

The boy, still amused, regarded him from the ground, then sprang to his feet in a swift movement. "So come," he said, "observe."

Michaels followed him as he clambered easily over the jagged remains of the wall that blocked their way. Footing was slippery and difficult; the young ensign dug his nails into the crevices in the rocks and pulled.

On the other side of the wall a group of boys of various ages sat in a ring. A circle was drawn in the dirt within their circle, and a fire blazed at the center of that. In Michaels's mind there again stirred hopes of having stumbled upon some weird religious cult. But the boys seemed too boisterous and casual to fit such a scenario.

They laughed and joked loudly as their leader told of pouncing and landing on the intruder, and added, with mock gravity, "He has come to observe us." Michaels stood to one side awkwardly, unsure of what attitude to assume. The other boys laughed, and turned back to what they had been doing.

One boy—he looked about twelve—held colorfully painted stones in his hands, and shook them, and let them fall in the circle drawn in the dirt. An older boy spun a bundle of short sticks in the air, and let them fall on and among the rocks. The pattern thus formed meant nothing to Michaels. It seemed to mean a great deal to the gang; there were whistles for the winners of the wager, jeers for the losers.

Michaels watched intently as a few more hands

were thrown, trying to get a grasp on the rules of the game.

"Want to play?" the leader asked him abruptly. Once again, Michaels felt all eyes in the room upon him.

For the few weeks he had been aboard the *Enterprise,* he had felt tremendous pride in his uniform, in his long-coveted assignment to a starship; these were the symbols of manhood he had sought his whole life to attain. But there was a glamour and an elegance to the swagger of this Boacan boy, his opposite, this grimy, tattered hooligan, that he knew could never be his. It caused him to feel a sharp pain. He straightened. "I'm ready when you are."

This resulted in more whistles and catcalls. The stones were placed in Michaels's hand, the other boy took the sticks, and the game began, a blur of color, and smoke from the fire, and crisscrossed patterns that Michaels could barely follow. Somehow, the pieces never rolled into the fire and somehow, Michaels sensed, every throw worsened his position. The jeers of the gang confirmed it. "Well?" he snapped at last.

The leader sat back on his heels. "Whoo. Keep to flying in the sky, spaceboy. This game is not for you. Never has anyone lost so much, so fast."

Michaels's hand moved to the money pouch at his waist. They had been given some of the local currency, been urged by the captain to use it sparingly. "How much do you want?" he said.

The other boy shook his head. "No, spaceboy. No, you'd be too easy to rob blind. You do not even know enough to demand that *you* get to throw the sticks at alternate turns. You keep your money. Let the others get on with the game."

The game recommenced, and Michaels quickly sensed he had become invisible to the other boys.

"Does the revolutionary council know about gangs like yours?" he asked the leader sharply. "Or do you work for them?"

"Gangs like mine?" the boy laughed. "I think the council has more things to worry about than how we spend our time. For them, the gangs that have little street wars are a problem. Hard to control. But us? We are peaceful men." He grinned.

"But if there are many groups like yours," Michaels said, excited, "if you were coordinated, don't you think you'd be a threat to the Council of Youngers?"

The boy's grin faded, and he stood appraising him. "I'll say it again. I have no quarrel with the Council of Youngers. *They,* at least, don't try to tell me what to do."

He turned abruptly, and once again scaled the jutting projection of the fallen wall. Michaels, uncertain what to do, at last followed him. He found the boy waiting on the other side.

"Well," the boy said, "since you say you are here to observe, do you want to meet some of the people of Boaco Six? Would you like the grand tour of the poor neighborhoods of this city?"

Michaels nodded slowly and followed him out into the sunlight.

Chapter Eight

KIRK STOOD BY and watched as each of his men left or was led away from the public square to explore this new world. The Boacans were making an effort to afford every man a chance to use his area of expertise. Rizzuto was taken off to receive the council's official account of the revolution and to be shown plans for more museums, libraries, and cultural archives. The government was obviously anxious to disprove rumors that they intended to wipe out traditional culture here.

The agriculturalist was met by a voluble young minister, who lectured him as they wandered off to view model farms, and to witness the use of new machinery, and new methods of irrigation and crop rotation that were being introduced. Most of the planet could live well, generally, off the sinfully abundant flora and fauna. But there were pockets that were barren and parched, or burned and flattened by the war. Those areas were now being reached, and refugees from them moved to the city or to new farming communities. And nutrition *was* being taught . . .

Quite suddenly, Kirk realized only he and Spock remained in the public square.

"Well, Mr. Spock," Kirk said, turning to his first officer. "It appears the Boacans have abandoned us."

"On the contrary, Captain. The council's new minister of justice is to meet me here shortly, to explain the intricacies of their new legal code. I am sure that your presence would also be welcome—"

"No," Kirk replied quickly. "I don't think that will be necessary." Truth be told, he was less interested in hearing about the council's new laws than in seeing what life underneath those laws was like for the people of Boaco Six. He wanted to see more of the capital city itself as well. "I believe I'll do a little exploring—on my own."

Spock nodded. "As you wish."

Kirk left his first officer and wandered out onto the streets of Boa. Much as he had instructed young Michaels to do, he spoke with the people, observing the arrest of a thief, the relocation of a homeless child, the stomping and dancing of a wedding party.

Several times, Kirk felt that he was being followed. It was an instinctive feeling, one that caused the hair on his arms and on the back of his neck to stand on end. He turned several times, but in the bustle of the street, it was difficult to be sure who his shadow was. Several times he caught sight of an old man with a cap on and gaunt hollowed cheeks, walking with a rather dumpy young man. He wondered if they were following him, or merely following a similar course as his. Were they sent by the council to keep tabs on him? He stared at them fixedly, making sure they were aware of it, then wheeled off abruptly down an alleyway. They did not follow.

The alley led to a business section of the city. Kirk

browsed through the busy marketplace, with its haphazard rows of stalls run by people selling hollowed gourds as bowls, and dried fruit, and leather pelts, and freshly killed game, ready for roasting. The traditional handmade objects were exquisite, the few trinkets for sale from other worlds were junky and cheap.

Some older people, in tents, practiced folk medicine, and called out to sick or elderly passersby, promising comfort and cures.

As merchants in their stalls saw Kirk pass, they came alive and called out to him, singing the praises of their wares, begging his patronage in curious and broken English. Kirk was reminded of an account he had read when preparing for this mission, of an early Federation explorer of the Boacan system. He had been treated as a half-deity, capable of helping or destroying the people. The deference people were showing Kirk now, the desperate edge to the stall keepers' cries, made him uneasy, made him feel more like a colonial overlord than a visiting dignitary or tourist.

A thin seven-year-old boy in ragged clothing suddenly leapt out in front of him. Earthenware candle holders were in the boy's arms and strapped to his back. "Buy candle holders. Buy candle holders, spaceman," the boy urged. "Good buy. Brighten your home."

"Sorry," Kirk began, "but I don't think so . . ."

Abruptly, a small girl of five or so, carrying similar goods, pushed in front of the boy and tugged at the hem of Kirk's shirt.

"Better buy," she piped. "I sell cheaper."

The boy made a face and pointed at the clay candle

holder in his competitor's small fist. "Poor quality," he said. "Cracks in the heat."

"Better buy," the girl said again, determinedly. "I sell cheaper."

Kirk reached into the small pouch of money he'd been handed by Noro when they left the museum. Each member of the landing party was supplied with some of the newly minted currency, enough to get around with. He bought one candle holder from each child and showered into each eager palm a clattering of bright Boacan coins. The children exclaimed and ran off in opposite directions to crouch and count their earnings. Kirk gave the candle holders to an old man in a stall as he passed.

At dusk, he observed a religious ceremony in the clearing near the woods where they had first arrived. An old woman led the wailing and chanting. It was an ancient ritual, alien and strange sounding. Cacophonous moans that Kirk did not think he could duplicate if he tried. He did not understand the words, but from cultural history tapes, he knew the meaning behind them. These people were praying to their old god, the God of Light. On Boaco Six, light was the life force, the river running through each person, binding him to his world. Pitch darkness was a thing most feared.

They prayed to Azar, the larger star of their system and the one closer to them. They prayed to Alil, the farther star, the 'younger brother' of the first. They prayed to their planet's three moons, the Mirror Maidens, the guardians of the city of Boa. The religion was slightly different on different parts of the planet.

Do they really believe? Or is this just a link with

tradition and culture and preextraterrestrial times, a mainstay in times of chaos?

The people, dressed in traditional garb, did not challenge Kirk's presence at their ceremony, did not really seem to see him. He hung at the outskirts and crouched low, as the people buried their faces in the orange earth and wept.

And when the old woman had finished wailing, they picked themselves up, dusted off their clothes, and sauntered back toward the city, laughing and talking quietly.

Spock was left in the public square for over an hour after the others had left. He stood, erect but relaxed, his hands clasped behind his back, and wondered if the Boacans, in their well-meaning disorganization, had forgotten about him.

At last he made out a figure walking toward him, a shriveled frame of a man, an ancient creature such as one rarely encountered on this world. The man bowed and introduced himself as Mayori, the minister of justice.

Spock mused, as he accompanied Mayori to the Hall of Justice, that the man's situation must be delicate and strange; the one elder statesman in a government of young people. They discussed the scantily documented new legal code, in the dusty and crumbling hall. Spock wondered how seriously the standardization of the legal code was being taken. Perhaps the council had shunted the ministry of justice onto this old-timer precisely because it was of little interest to them.

Mayori volunteered to show him the new rehabilitation centers and penal camps; this seemed to Spock an excellent way to test his hypothesis. The way these centers were run would reflect the man, and the system. They set out in a cramped Romulan-designed air-skimmer. During the 'long and bumpy ride, Mayori told him much of the history of his life.

"The revolutionary struggle on Boaco Six is very old. Though you would not know it to hear Irina, Tamara Angel, Noro, and some of the others tell it." He had laughed, a dry sound, like crackling leaves. "We have been fighting to free our planet for centuries, despite cruel opposition from the combined forces of the tyrants like Markor and Puil, and their friends in the Federation. The freedom movement in its current form started fifty years ago. I am the last of that old vanguard. The others, my friends, my sisters and brothers in arms, were slain or tortured . . . or met with some even less savory fate."

Spock noted a facial tic as Mayori spoke.

"I have spent years in prison," he went on, "living in excrement, in crowded cells packed full of men who forgot what light was, who felt that our two suns, Azar and Alil, and the Mirror Maidens, were lost from them forever. The stench, the fear, the monotony, as we spilled over each other month after month in the darkness, was overwhelming. Political prisoners were crowded in with cutthroats and psychotics. There never seemed to be enough air to breathe. I would be dragged from the cell by the hair at times, beaten and whipped, locked in Puil's majestic zoo for weeks at a time, naked, without food, until I screamed like the animals. I and my friends were wracked with electric currents, sliced by laser guns . . . of course, all the most sophisticated torture devices were provided by the Federation of Planets."

Here, Spock felt it necessary to respond. "I do not

doubt the truth of your horrific account, Mayori. And I am aware that the Federation gave funds and military aid to the former rulers of Boaco Six, men of little moral virtue. But, surely you must realize that the Federation does not design torture devices. It could not know that its money and equipment were being used for such purposes."

Mayori gazed at him steadily. It was a look, not of bitterness, but of sadness . . . or amusement? "No, of course not," he said softly. "Why should the Federation have chosen to know what the whole galaxy knew?"

Spock defended the Federation on this score, but with little conviction. "Then, Mayori," he said, "you stayed in prison until the revolution came?"

The minister of justice shook his old, scarred, chapped head. "Much of my adolescence and my young years were spent in jail. But they released me on several occasions, and friends helped me to escape on others. Guards, judges could be bribed. . . . I got out one time, after nine years, to discover that my parents and my family had all been killed. I just stood staring at the charred, fallen remains of our ancestral home. Neighbors told me of how it had come about. My family had already been under surveillance because of my 'subversive' activities. Then a sister of mine was accused of links with revolutionaries on the other landmass, and of disseminating classified government information. The government sent in its army and secret police. All the women in my family were dishonored before they were killed, the men emasculated, the children crushed against trees. Even cousins of ours, in a small farming community many miles away, were wiped out . . ."

His eyes grew distant, then focused on Spock sharply. "I had a wife and four children in later years. Until twelve years ago. The revolutionary network was better organized. We would be smuggled from town to town in times of danger. And victory seemed so near . . . But as revolutionary fervor grew, the dictators grew more frightened, more vindictive . . . and there are always stool pigeons and traitors . . . well, my wife and children are gone too." He looked down. "It was a good racket for the government, you know, wiping out prestigious families or entire poor villages and confiscating their land and property for the government's profit. And many of these younger friends of mine have been disowned by their families. So the revolution, the council now, is 'family' for many of them." A wry smile cracked the old face. "As it is for me, I am the wise old 'grandfather' of the council, I suppose."

Spock flew on with him in silence, as the air-skimmer sputtered over the hill-peaks and treetops, and speculated about what a penal colony under this man's jurisdiction would be like. The Federation reports had said that, though the oldest of the leaders of Boaco Six, Mayori was the most radical, the most distrustful of the Federation. And 'penal camps' could often mean cruel places of internment for those who gambled wrong, and backed the wrong side in a revolution. For a man who had known such a violent bloody past as had Mayori, running the camps would be a fine opportunity for a vendetta against the people who had supported his former oppressors.

The air-skimmer screeched to a halt on a sloping runway near the first penal colony they visited. Spock had found it smaller than he had expected. A twenty-foot-tall barrier of impenetrable plastic stretched around the penal colony, forming an opaque wall. The lush jungle vegetation which grew all around outside the barrier could still be seen. Inside was a series of huts and roads forming a small villagelike community. And there was farming land, clearly demarcated into plots by lines and low walls, which lay beyond the huts. A few men could be seen lazily tilling or weeding their plots, or taking soil samples, or spreading the eggs of small, helpful, insectlike creatures, which when they hatched would naturally turn over the soil and eat small predators. From atop the rickety runway, Old Mayori pointed out the farming plots and explained different kinds of activity. Spock helped him to slowly, painfully, climb down and stand alone on firm ground.

They walked toward the cluster of huts. Several taller administration buildings stood at the center. Young guards with rifles stood before these buildings, and they saluted Mayori as he and Spock passed. But otherwise, the prison inmates wandered freely, worked or rested as they pleased, with seemingly no supervision. They dressed casually and gathered in groups before their homes to talk or shoot dice.

"They are given some rations," Mayori explained, "and farm for the rest of what they need. These people have led recent rebellions against our new government. We know that the Federation of Planets funds and encourages their activities. But we believe also that many of them have turned against us because they are frightened, and do not know how they will make their livelihood under the new order. They stay here and work, until they give us a solemn promise to cease in their efforts to destabilize the government. Then they are allowed to leave."

Spock's eyebrows shot up. "A promise? And then you let them go?"

His guide nodded. "There is something you must understand about Boaco Six, Mr. Spock. We take our oaths very seriously here. As, I believe, you people from the planet Vulcan do. The old dictators here used to torture men, simply to extract from them a promise that they would cease in their revolutionary activities. Many died rather than give such a promise."

A group of men walked by with farm implements slung over their shoulders. They eyed Mayori and Spock with more interest than hostility.

"Of course," Mayori continued, "some of these men may break their word if we release them, and stir up more trouble. If they do, they will be interned again. I believe that this is the best system, to try to give men the benefit of the doubt. Though I admit it's not the most efficient." He gestured toward a fat, squat administration building. "We also have educational facilities here, so that the men who leave here will be able to read and write, and will be trained in a skill other than farming, if they wish."

"And propaganda, here and in the children's schools, plays no part in your 'education' process?"

"We stress the benefits of the revolution, certainly. But men are not penalized here for disagreement or skepticism. It is not the kind of brainwashing the Federation claims we practice." He smiled. "In fact, we find it informative to let the men speak out freely in discussion groups. It keeps us informed about our enemies' own brands of propaganda, what they wish Boacans to believe about our government. Our main goal, though, is to provide these men with the skills necessary to enable them to reintegrate with Boacan society."

They reboarded their clumsy flying machine, and

Mayori told Spock of the larger internment camp they would visit next, for henchmen and members of the secret police of the former dictators. The word of those men had been found to be less trustworthy, and many of them had been interned for life. Their wives and families could come and live with them if they wished, and could, of course, come and go as they pleased.

"Many of those men are afraid to return to their native towns and villages. Their neighbors know of their past activities. They are linked to atrocities against their kinsmen—they have achieved infamy. If they return to their communities, many fear they would be murdered in their beds."

"So," Spock said somewhat skeptically, "you imply that they prefer to serve a prison sentence?"

"Some, perhaps. Believe me or not, as you wish."

Spock was reluctant to believe that Mayori's word, and what he was being shown, told the whole story of the prison system of Boaco Six. He wondered, even if what they had seen was typical, if a system of such laxity could survive if the counterrevolutionary movement, which brewed in some parts of the planet, was to gain force, supplied by either the Federation or Boaco Eight. Mayori's 'Honor System' might not stand the strain.

Still, he was impressed, with both the man, and what he seemed to be trying to create—especially after their visit to the next camp.

This one was larger than the other they had seen, and was heavily guarded. Mayori explained why the men here had been singled out; they'd been convicted of monstrous crimes against the people of Boaco Six. "Torture in the cities. Genocide of small tribes in the jungle, on the islands. Always under the old government's jurisdiction . . . though to what degree a man like Puil could control his secret police is an interesting question. There were many 'strongmen' within the police and army. The others here are the petty officers, lackeys of the fallen regime."

Spock assumed that those who had been responsible for Mayori's torture and the destruction of his family were here also. He did not ask.

Mayori stated that many in the council desired the death of these men. But he did not, and as minister of justice, the final decision rested with him. This was a reformist institution, like the others.

From what Spock could see, the facility was well run, the living conditions decent. Always fascinated as he was by humanoid psychology, Spock studied old Mayori as they boarded the air-skimmer at dusk for their trip back to the city. He questioned him as the craft wheezed and sputtered into the air.

"I wonder, Mayori, if you could explain something to me. You have as great a reason as any for wishing to exact retribution from these men. What motivates you to act as you do now?"

"After a lifetime of struggle, Mr. Spock, I have come to terms with my anger and grief. I find inner peace through revenge."

"Revenge?"

"Yes. The clemency we show these men. The reasonableness, the fairness of the system. The humane treatment they receive. That is my revenge for the barbarity of what they did to me."

Chapter Nine

KIRK ASKED FOR no report at the end of the first day. The *Enterprise* men were given a trough of water to bathe in. It looked black and slimy, but was surprisingly invigorating, left their skin tingling and clean.

Ensign Michaels seemed quiet and uncertain that evening. Spock also sat off by himself, lost in thought. Kirk had hoped to confer with his first officer, get his opinion on a few things. But he chose, as usual, not to disturb the Vulcan in a contemplative mood.

McCoy asked to speak with him, led him to a corner of the bungalow, and told him of the medical help he had dispensed that day, at the clinic and on the *Enterprise.*

"Maybe I was out of line, Jim. But I can't say I'm sorry that I did it. I was a healer, faced with five emergencies at once. And you know better than I that this planet doesn't correspond to the pristine, untampered with, developing model."

"Agreed, Bones. Starfleet procedure on how to handle a damaged world like this is a little blurry. And they've authorized me to use my discretion in such matters on this mission. So no, I don't object to your pitching in." He shook his head. "But I *do* object to your beaming people up to the *Enterprise,* and more personnel down, without checking with me. No matter what the emergency. It's not just the development of the planet we have to consider. It's the delicacy of our situation."

"Of course, Jim, you're right. But it was just Christine who beamed down, and she's a trooper. And you know, it's a funny thing. We're so worried about the government here spreading propaganda against us. But I think the work I did today was the best possible propaganda *for* us. I think it made these people see Starfleet in a very different light."

"All right then, Bones. Well-done."

"Oh, and Captain?"

"Yes?"

"If I'm faced with a similar situation tomorrow?"

Kirk smiled, and clapped him on the shoulder. "I guess I can count on you to use your medical judgment."

Both men turned in for the night.

The second day brought investigations farther afield. McCoy, along with the agriculturalist and the education specialist, was flown farther out into the bush. Rizzuto, the historian, was flown on the planet's one "ocean-crossing air ferry" to the landmass on the opposite side of the planet, where an archive and a civic center were being built. The aircrafts were obviously of Klingon and Romulan design, and no attempt was made to hide this fact. But questions about the number of air- and seacrafts acquired from the enemies of the Federation received evasive answers. The aircrafts were quite primitive, corresponding roughly to solar powered planes from Earth's twenty-second century.

Primitive weapons and machines, manufactured and sold on all sides to these developing worlds; madness, Kirk thought. *But the way the game is played. The way the balance of power is maintained.*

"Mr. Spock," he asked, when his first officer returned from another session with Mayori, "why, do you think, they've taken for themselves the name of the 'Council of Youngers'?"

"It would seem, Captain, an ironic twist to this planet's traditional reverence for the old and wise. That *is* one aspect of the culture they seem to be out to change."

Kirk nodded. "A culture they share with Boaco Eight, isn't that so? Sun worshipping, reverence for the old, and the native language on this solar system's other inhabited planet are similar, aren't they?"

"Yes, Captain. Rizzuto would know more about it than I. But the two planets' cultures are similar enough that it is clear that one populated the other in the distant past. This is borne out by the ruins of ancient temples dedicated to the gods of light that have been found in this world in the western sea—"

"Which haven't been properly excavated?"

"No, sir. Not by any government here, past or present. But they are very similar in structure to the vast temple ruins on Boaco Eight; immense in size, complex in structure. They indicate a fascinating, and most sophisticated culture. We don't know on which world it originated. But one Boacan planet *must* have been capable of space travel, millennia ago, and colonized the other."

"What's your take on Boaco Eight, Spock? The people running it now?"

"They . . . are not as corrupt or cruel as those who used to rule on *this* world. But they are hardly democratic or enlightened leaders. The Federation has been on close terms with them, as you know, since the revolution here."

"Sending the *Enterprise* on a mission to Boaco Six, with no stopover at Boaco Eight, signals somewhat of a shift in Federation policy, wouldn't you say?" Kirk asked.

"More of an experiment, Captain—one Boaco Eight, in all likelihood, is not happy about. They fear the ruling council on this world will try to spread revolution to theirs. And they fear the Federation will abandon them—they, after all, have no argea-producing plants on their world."

Kirk nodded. It seemed clear Starfleet would have to juggle feelings of paranoia on both worlds in order to keep them at peace with each other—and the Federation.

Kirk asked for reports that evening from all his men. The older officers were cautious, restrained in their comments. Advances were definitely being made on this world; changes were generally for the better. People in obscure and distressed areas were receiving education, medicine, and food; the system was practical, if unorganized, and seemed to be working. It could be called a model for underdeveloped planets. Of course, it was impossible to say if what had been seen in two days represented the situation on the whole planet. But the contrast to, say, five years earlier seemed staggering.

"Do you know how many babies used to die here?"

McCoy was almost accusatory in his tone. "How many healthy adults were cut down by simple curable diseases? At last, the doctors here are fighting back. Granted, they're understaffed, lacking supplies. I'm not saying the battle is won. But the strides they're making in health education . . . it's remarkable, what they seem to have accomplished."

"It is remarkable, sir, it's a world in transition!" Michaels's eyes were bright with enthusiasm. Restraint was not of interest to him. "The people are still going through some hard times, but they have faith in the council. They *shudder* when Markor, and Puil, and the other old rulers are mentioned. We should ally ourselves with this planet, the new regime, help it along!"

Kirk tried to suppress a smile. But he didn't try too hard. "I thought you distrusted the rebel council, Mr. Michaels."

"But, sir, they're protecting the culture, they're popular . . ."

"The intergalactic situation, Ensign. I thought that was of primary importance to you."

"But it's a *good* planet, Captain. It's right. You can feel it."

"Very well, Ensign. Mr. Spock, how 'right' would you say the judicial system here is?"

"Judging from what I've seen, Captain, they're heading in a productive direction. Tolerant of criticism, up to the point of insurrection. Merciful penal camps with an emphasis on the rehabilitation of prisoners. The ones that I saw . . . impressed me a great deal. They contrasted sharply with the torture chambers of Puil. There is respect for private property here, and for freedom of travel.

"But justice seems conducted in a rather haphazard fashion, here. It is difficult to find anything written down, any codified laws. What I have seen may, in fact, be atypical. In fact, what all of us have seen may be the equivalent of what they used to call a cardboard town, a Potemkin village."

"Exactly, Mr. Spock. So the issue now is, do we recommend that the Federation send a *real* investigatory team here to do months of in-depth research? And obviously, that depends on whether we think it's to the Federation's advantage to have good relations with Boaco Six. And *that,* gentlemen, does depend greatly on the intergalactic situation. Comments?"

Rizzuto, the historian, spoke. "Captain, I've found a lot that I admire on this world. Obviously, on a planet that's been interfered with so much by all sides, for centuries, the Prime Directive becomes a moot point. But the present government *is* making an effort to keep the planet evolving independently, with its own culture. And yet, we know they're being influenced. And it's the same for all of us—they're incredibly open and friendly, but when we start asking questions about Klingon and Romulan aid, they clam up."

"Even the townspeople don't want to talk about that," Michaels admitted, reluctantly.

Kirk shifted on his cot. The bungalow had seemed the most private place for a meeting. "And yet we know that the aid has been substantial. Boaco Six wants to claim neutrality and make deals on all sides. For such a planet, in this quadrant, that's virtually impossible. Well? Are they playing coy with us? Are they Klingon dupes?"

There was a silence.

"Impossible to say, Captain, at this time," Spock said finally.

Kirk waved his hand in a vague gesture of impatience. "All right, then. Tomorrow, one last day of investigations, and in the evening, I'll arrange a meeting with the Council of Youngers. Then we'll get down to business."

Chapter Ten

KIRK FELT GOOD as he walked out into the warm night air. The city street seemed to pulse with people and music, and shafts and columns of light poured down, piercing the orange clouds. Looking out, far out over the lush forest, he could see the burgundy brilliance of a double sunset.

He flipped open his communicator. "Kirk to *Enterprise.*"

"Lieutenant Uhura here, Captain."

"Lieutenant. Everything under control?"

"All quiet here, sir."

"Status of the Boacan patients McCoy had beamed aboard?"

"Sickbay reports they are all in stable condition."

"Good. Uhura, I've received permission from the Boacan government for a limited number of people from our ship to come down on shore leave. Say, six people. I'll give you the new coordinates—they're different from the ones that we used."

"Yes, Captain. I'll notify the next six people on the shore leave roster."

"And tell them to be careful, use discretion while they're down here, Lieutenant. The situation here is still sensitive."

"Yes, sir."

Kirk gave her the coordinates for the city's center, then signed off. This was a tricky situation still, but he trusted his crew, and they'd been too long without shore leave.

A mild breeze eddied through the tropical evening air. The soft wet earth no longer felt so strange beneath his boots; he no longer noticed the lack of the even carpeting of his starship's decks and rooms and corridors, was no longer so conscious of the stillness that had replaced her hums and whirrs and tremors, the living feel of the ship all around him. Well, not stillness, exactly, he corrected himself, as he watched three small children scuffle over a shiny bauble on a piece of string—but a very different kind of living environment.

He himself could never feel truly at home, when planetside. He felt a restless anxiety every few hours for the *Enterprise,* circling the planet, though he reassured himself by remembering she was under Scotty's capable guidance.

But something about this particular world satisfied him, lulled him, and he let himself be lulled. It was not Eden, was no land of innocence. But it hadn't lost the excitement, the idealism, the comic strangeness of innocence; it was a rich, exotic world, full of life, and Kirk let himself be absorbed by its rhythms.

He had gotten to know the southern quarter of the city of Boa fairly well, picked his way among the ruins and thatched huts.

Music poured out from under the sagging eaves of a

tavern, and Kirk suddenly became aware of how parched his throat was. A drop of Boacan brandy would not be amiss. Perhaps he could bring some back for McCoy; the doctor appreciated that kind of elemental medicine.

Kirk pushed aside the dried red and purple vines that hung from the top bar of the door frame, and entered the smoke-filled room. There was laughter, and the tapping and sliding and clinking of glasses of brandy. And wooden cups and bowls of brandy. A little boy in a darkened corner appeared absorbed in drinking brandy out of an old boot.

Old men were playing a giddy fast dance tune on drums and lutelike instruments. One instrument was long and ovular, strung with eight strings and tapering at both ends. It took three men to play it.

Young people clapped and danced and swayed with the music. Kirk slid onto a stool by a table that projected out of the round bar like a peninsula. He ordered a tumbler full of the black sparkling spirit. When the drink arrived, he took a handful of coins out of his small leather purse and slid them across the counter.

He cradled the tumbler in his hand, turned it, and watched the liquid catch the light, like a black emerald. He quaffed it in one gulp and instantly regretted it. His eyes stung and his throat burned. *Not quite a native yet,* he thought, and ordered another.

"Hey, sailor! You will buy me a drink maybe, yes?" Tamara Angel had emerged from the crowd and was leaning her elbows on the table beside him, chin in hand, smiling.

Kirk smiled at her awkward rendering of the old line. "Make that two," he called down to the barkeep.

Tamara was still in her fatigues. But her thick black hair fell loosely about her shoulders, and her maroon eyes danced. Her dark skin flickered in the lights of the bar. "We have a theory here, Captain, about why the Federation is so angered by our revolution. It is not so much because they fear the loss of our argea—other planets have trees enough to supply those needs. It is because they fear the loss of our brandy."

"Wars have been fought for lesser things," Kirk said, handing her a tumbler.

"You must know. You know your history better than I could claim to. Here is mud going in your eye," she said agreeably. The Terran clichés sounded quaint and strange in her mouth. She gulped the drink down without blinking.

Kirk nursed his. The best thing about the brandy, it seemed, was the warm flush it brought with passing time. Perhaps his personal charm would *not* be for nothing here. "How did you become involved in all this, Tamara? What is this revolution to you?" In his mind, the words resonated ironically. *What's a pretty girl like you doing in a revolution like this?*

"I'll have another," she yelled loudly, and turned back to him. "It is simply my whole life, Captain . . ."

"Jim, please."

"It is my whole life, Jim. The only thing that makes sense. I was brought up to respect, almost revere your Federation. But I have visited some of the Federated Planets, and I did not always like what I saw."

Kirk saw a point that needed to be clarified. "There are differences among the worlds, certainly. The Federation does not have absolute authority over its members. It is a coalition, based on the idea that we are stronger standing together than apart."

"Then it has no moral basis, upholds no code of values?"

"I didn't say that. Only that each planet is self-governed under a different system. Its culture, its history affect that system. But the Federation has rules and values, shared among its members, and it withholds membership from worlds that are too corrupt, or at too early a stage of development . . . that is why this world was never admitted when it was ruled by the men you deposed."

"But it was aided!"

"It was aided, and there were hopes that eventually it would evolve into a more enlightened system—"

"What if it has?" Tamara challenged him.

"Is that an application for membership?" Kirk asked nonchalantly.

"Is that an offer of membership?" she replied.

Kirk smiled. "I'm afraid, Tamara, we'll never get anywhere if we keep playing these coy, evasive games."

She sighed. "You are right, Jim. But it is our job to be evasive with each other. How I wish we could be more . . . direct."

Whoa, back off, Kirk thought. Where exactly was this leading? What had they been talking about before? "You were telling me about yourself, Tamara. About how you became involved in the movement here . . ."

"Ah, yes. The story of my life. Well then. My family was quite well-off under Puil. Illustrious, even respected by the people. A family of scholars, writers, poets . . . a family that dabbled in the rhetoric of reform and populism. And was tolerated, because we knew enough not to go too far. I wanted something more to have, more to do. I felt something more was necessary."

The jagged scar of a knife wound on her arm caught the light; it went up past her elbow joint and disappeared under the rolled-up sleeve of her fatigues. *She's so impossibly young for this,* Kirk thought.

As if reading his mind, Tamara went on. "I have no regrets for anything I have done. I have been disowned by my parents and uncles. I have a younger brother who thinks the revolution is very wonderful. I see him sometimes. But I have a new family now—those I have fought beside. The tearing down, the killing, and the pain are over now. We have only to build, to create." Her voice took on a hard edge. "If we are given the chance to do these things. If our world is not distorted again by outsiders."

She wanted to keep the talk strong; he wouldn't mince words.

"The people of Boaco Eight are not sure that rebuilding your planet is the only thing you have on your agenda. They don't like the people you do business with. They don't like your links with subversives on their world. They don't like the way you're arming yourself. They think you're preparing for a civil war within this solar system."

Tamara's face showed contempt. "The government of Boaco Eight will express any fear the Federation tells it is appropriate, will jump through a hoop if the Federation so requires. As for the *people* of that world, they are hardly at issue, here. Or ever, for the Federation."

"Perhaps you don't like their government? Perhaps you'd like to give them a new one?"

Tamara Angel smiled to ease the tension. "Perhaps

I do not want to walk into a trap, Jim. I tell you we simply want to coexist with all the neighboring worlds, to stay neutral in galactic conflicts, and do business with whoever shows us good faith and goodwill and can give us what we need . . ."

"Even a renegade system like Orion? They're worthy business partners?"

"I tell you we are simply surviving. You must form your own opinion. What do you plan to report to your Federation about us?"

Kirk considered for a moment before responding. "From what we've seen, your world is heading in an encouraging direction. I don't know if we can trust you. But I'd like to meet with your whole Council of Youngers tomorrow. Pending that meeting, I believe my report will be favorable. I'll recommend that relations be increased, that research teams come and pick up where we left off. How does that sound?"

"It is a very welcome sound, Jim. I hope this means that you will stop sabotaging our supply lines, prejudicing Boaco Eight against us, arming our enemies here . . ."

"Can you prove any of those charges?"

"No, but I stand by them. I am glad that you are giving our world a chance. That is all we need to prove ourselves."

A group of young men came up to the bar, shoving each other and laughing. "Hey, Tamara Angel!" called one. "You are going wild, girl. Maybe you have fallen in love with Starfleet glamour."

"Maybe, Rigo," she called back. "Do you have something better to offer me?"

Not the usual manner of a minister dealing with the public, Kirk mused.

"Oh no, I have nothing! No warp drive, no photon torpedoes. No matter-antimatter charge. Ah, Tamara Angel, I know you will never be mine." The boy pretended to sob into the shoulder of one of his buddies, and their whole group laughed. "Take her, Starfleet man. She is lost to our cause."

The whole bar seemed to be in on the joke now. The old men stopped their pulsing fluttering tune and switched to a slower one, recognizable in any culture as romantic. A toothless man squatting on the floor laid aside his drums and began to sing, in ancient unfamiliar words resembling the wailing of the religious ceremony Kirk had observed in the clearing.

"What is he saying?" he asked Tamara Angel.

"It is a very old song," she said, slightly embarrassed. "It speaks of Azar, our closest star. It says, 'May the light of Azar flow through you, spark your love, flow through me, bind us together.' I think they are having some fun at our expense, Jim."

Kirk grinned. "You could be right at that, Tamara."

"It is so unfair! After all, Jim, we are very serious people. We are having a very serious meeting, are we not?"

"Guess they just don't understand."

Two of the boys shouted over the song, "Tamara Angel! The soldier of Boa! The toast of every quadrant!"

Tamara splashed some brandy in their direction. "I'll soldier you! I'll teach you to insult the minister of interplanetary relations!"

The boys hooted. "Interplanetary relations. And you are having some now, yes?"

Laughter filled the tavern. Tamara was off her stool, half ready to fight the leader of the boys.

"Tamara Angel!" This was a new voice that spoke. It was deep, serious, and it sliced through the merry atmosphere of the bar. It came from a tall boy who filled the door frame. The talk, laughter, and music died away; all heads turned to look at him. Kirk recognized him as Iogan, the minister of public welfare, to whom he'd been introduced that afternoon. A grim young man he had seemed, and still seemed.

"Tamara Angel," he said again. "I must speak to you."

Tamara put down her tumbler, and the crowd parted to let her reach the door. She and Iogan disappeared behind the red-purple vines. Two armed guards appeared in their place, and they glared in Kirk's direction. The people in the bar turned to their drinks, began to talk quietly, and the music softly commenced again.

When Tamara returned in five minutes time, her expression was hard and bitter. She held her head high as she walked toward Kirk.

"Well, Captain, it appears we have misjudged you and your men. We thought you were here to learn about us. We thought yours was a mission of importance. But it appears that you were only a decoy. A distraction from what the Federation really had planned."

"I don't understand."

"Perhaps you do and perhaps you do not. I do not know how extensive your orders have been." Her voice was filled with disgust. "But in case you are being truthful, I shall explain to you my meaning. While we have been hosting you here with trust, Irina, our minister of relations with Boaco Eight, was on a mission to that planet. And one of their leading ministers was coming here, to meet with our council. We planned to let you see him here, to demonstrate that the situation in our solar system is improving . . ." Her voice trailed off in disappointment.

Iogan stood beside her. "Captain Kirk, we have just decoded a message from Irina's ship, which was escorting the ship of the minister from Boaco Eight. The minister's ship was just attacked and demolished —everyone on board was killed. Irina's crew was able to identify the attacking vessel as a small ship of Starfleet design and make. It fired wildly and erratically, and crippled the ship of Irina, our comrade in arms. She will not be able to make it home to Boaco Six."

Tamara cut in. "But nevertheless, Boaco Eight will say that *we* instigated the attack, that we killed their minister. When it is the Federation! Always out to sabotage all that we do! Killing Irina and destroying her mission of peace!"

Kirk spoke quietly but firmly. "That's impossible. The Federation would never do such a thing. You must be mistaken. It must have been some other type of vessel . . ."

"Are you a dupe, Captain?" Tamara demanded. "Or simply a very cunning spy? At any rate, we know her report to be accurate. Though we anticipate that Starfleet and the Federation will deny it. We will not mete out punishment against you and your men . . ."

Kirk's hand moved up ever so slightly toward the phaser at his waist.

She continued, ". . . but I am sorry to say that the *charade* of a meeting you requested with the Council of Youngers will not take place. Return to your starship. Leave our planet's orbit at once."

She and Iogan turned and left, one of the guards falling into step behind them, the other remaining to escort Kirk back to the bungalow. The captain looked around. The warm, amused atmosphere of the bar had given way to one of palpable suspicion and hatred.

Chapter Eleven

THE PIANO WAS a good one. A fine old Steinway, it had weathered centuries of use. It had traveled, by ship and air carrier, to every continent and climate on the planet Earth. Its journey had continued, out into the solar system of the star called Sol, and beyond. Its ivory keys had yellowed and chipped and been replaced, but the instrument itself had retained its integrity and excellence, its perfection of sound, the facility with which it could be played.

No other grand piano in the galaxy was as well preserved. Its owner had designed new systems, new chemicals for treating its wood and preserving it, for treating its strings, its joints, its polished pedals of brass. And now, the piano would outlast him. He could no longer preserve himself.

Flint sat with his eyes closed, and let his large hands wander the keyboard at their will. His thoughts did not wander over the infinite plane of time and existence. They were concentrated now on one of the lives he had lived, one of the personas he had chosen to be.

He had to be that man again, now, and through him create new kinds of music not conceived of in his time, create it light-years away from his original world.

As Johannes Brahms his hands moved again, his mind composed. His thoughts flowed again in German, and the faces, voices, scenes from that life swam in the music that he played.

He had not composed before becoming Brahms. Music had challenged him and intrigued him, yet he had not taken the time to master its principles, learn the rules of harmonics and relative keys, the capacity of sound of each of the major Western instruments.

He felt spurred on to try his hand at it in the nineteenth century largely through a love for the classical European traditions, which he saw threatened by experimenters. There were obscure composers he had heard over the last century who he wished to rediscover for the world through variations on their songs. There were ancient melodies, long forgotten, he could restore as his own. There were modern masters to whom he wanted to pay tribute . . . and there was the challenge of creating entirely on his own, expressing himself through the idiom of sound, for the first time in his life.

Another challenge was *becoming* a persona, a recognizable constant figure who must mature and age and pass away, as the man who created him slipped away to another country, safe and obscure. It was a challenge he had, by the 1800s, met many times before and mastered. His facility at disguise: producing a background, causing his features to age, arranging for a "burial" from which he would be absent, had become very great. And so Brahms had appeared, a young man playing the piano in various bordellos and taverns, developing his musical sensibility even as the veteran impostor who portrayed him learned the musical craft.

As a "twenty year old," he showed his work to Schumann, and the centuries he had spent hearing and imbibing the evolution of music were ghostly present in his work. Schumann wrote of him, praising, "a musician who is destined to voice ideally the spirit of his times, who reveals his mastery, not in a gradual unfolding, but like Athena springing full-armed from the head of Zeus . . . a young man over whose cradle the graces and Heroes have stood their watch. His name is Johannes Brahms . . ."

Sweet words, though they hinted at a young man oddly lacking youth, coming out of nowhere in full bloom. Schumann had been his patron, and with the onset of his madness and death, the widow, Clara, had remained a lifelong friend to Brahms.

As Brahms, Flint had never married and never fathered children. It was during a time of personal bitterness toward women that he assumed this identity, a time of anger at the impermanence of any love. He spent his gruff bachelor evenings drinking in the Red Hedgehog tavern. Stiff, blunt, antisocial, he kept himself from all intimate attachments that might hurt him, when they were severed.

The hands that wandered the piano keys paused, struck a cadence, and his right hand reached for the pen beside him on the piano bench. The pen was modern and leakproof, with modern ink, yet it was designed to look like an Old World quill, and its holder like an inkstand. Modern implements of writing had no elegance for Flint.

He scratched at the paper, connecting notes, filling

112

the bar with dots. A piano sonata was taking form beneath his hands. But the hands were stiff, there was an unfamiliar difficulty in the way they gripped the pen, the way they traveled the keys. And so at last he knew. This was how it felt to be aging, to have your mind conceive of things that your decaying body can barely execute. Time had claimed many before him, and now at last he felt its pull.

He threw off thoughts of his condition, focused his eyes on the wet ink on the page before him, and let his hands play over what they had just written. And again he was in Vienna, the music center in which this persona had given him a niche—such pleasure he had felt in being a part of it! There he had collected the autographed originals of so many great works; they were in his music library still. "Scraps of God," he said aloud, absently, and then scratched out part of what he had been writing.

Such awe he had felt for the masters who had been in that city before him, who in their brief spans of life had flashed a musical genius that amazed. After twenty years of professional life in music he had felt tall enough, despite the shadow of Beethoven, to show his first symphony. He had fought against the trend of the violent story telling of Wagner and Liszt, defended an older ideal of music, one of abstract emotion and thought. The piece he was composing now was true to that ideal, though it perhaps showed the more recent influence of Rigellian water music, as well.

He had watched, in his time, and after he had "passed away," the reactions of critics and the public to his work, their changing evaluation of what he had done, what he had achieved. He had been called both a sensualist and a calculating craftsman, a relic from the age of the symphony, and finally, decades later, he was recognized as one of the great masters, became one of the most performed.

This was one of his most amusing pastimes, to withdraw to the sidelines of history, and observe in anonymity how a man he had been was remembered. How and if his work survived. He had been some great men who were long forgotten, and others, like Brahms who were credited with the importance he knew they deserved. And they meant strange new things to people with every passing century.

The tough old hands ached with a strange new ache, yet Flint did not stop playing. Here in the act of creation he could forget Rayna, and all her predecessors. Here he could forget the end that awaited him, in his solitude, and feel a connection to something human . . .

Yet he was interrupted, by a robot's whirr. The small device hung in the air behind him, and he pulled himself back into the present and turned slowly to face it.

"Yes, M-7. Why do you disturb me when I am working?"

"It is necessary, signor," the robot replied in its flat dead voice, using the title he had programmed into it, the one with which he was most comfortable. "There is a call for you on the Priority One Starfleet channel. A member from the Federation ruling council wishes to address you."

This *was* urgent business. His sonata would have to be set aside until later. For the millionth time, Flint cursed these meddlesome lesser beings. How they inconvenienced him! Why had he restored contact with them? Why let this Priority One channel be installed?

"Very well, M-7. Tell the councilman I will join him presently."

The robot obediently floated out the door, to deliver the message. A few minutes later, Flint was in his salon, and standing before a large screen, face-to-face with a Tellarite. This creature had to be a minister of great stature, Flint knew, else he would not be serving on a Federation council. But his physical appearance repelled: the furry skin, the long snout in place of a nose, the hooflike hands, and beady eyes all seemed to denote a lesser intelligence. Still, Flint greeted him courteously. "If I can be of help to you, sir."

Unfortunately, Tellarites had a rude and temperamental manner, to match their rough appearance. "The Federation does not use the Priority One channel lightly, Mr. Flint. We used it because all other channels to your home were not being responded to."

"That is because I did not wish to be disturbed by anything less than an emergency. I prefer solitude, for my meditation and work."

"Well, what we have now is an emergency. You are surely the last in the galaxy to be informed. Relations between the United Federation of Planets and both the Klingon and Romulan empires have gone critical. We may not be able to avoid direct conflict much longer."

"Is that all?" Flint asked blithely. He had seen, he felt, larger crises than this.

"All?" the Tellarite repeated incredulously.

"What I mean to say is, how does this relate to me? How am I expected to help you in this matter?"

"Mr. Flint, the Federation is counting on your help. It is crucial that you design a new weapons system for us, with which our starships and battleships can be armed. If our enemies learned we had such a system, it would surely cause them to sue for peace."

Flint smiled wisely. "And what if it were to provoke them instead?"

"If they remain belligerent, then obviously, with such a system we will be better equipped to defend ourselves. We will have the advantage in battle. Mr. Flint, I appeal to your loyalty to the Federation in this. You are from the planet Earth. You must believe in the Federation, and all it stands for."

The argument was wearyingly familiar. Flint had had his loyalty appealed to before, fealty to generals, kings, empires and planets, leaders who planned to conquer eternity, who vanished in an instant. "I will design no weapons for you," he said firmly. "I have seen enough of war, and what men are capable of doing to each other. I have taken part in such violence before—I will not do so now. You must find another inventor."

"There is no one equal to yourself," the councilman said, stating the undeniable. "We need a system from you. You have said you intend to help the Federation. Do you renege on your promise?"

"I do not. I do help the Federation; science and the arts have profited by my knowledge. And if you want proof of my loyalty, recall that I have already designed a major system for Starfleet, my new cloaking device. If you are concerned about being attacked, ships armed with my device will have excellent camouflage. Let that suffice."

"It will not suffice!" the Tellarite snapped, barely holding his temper in check. After a moment, he said, "Mr. Flint, you are a hard man, and you force me to discuss matters which are dangerous to delve into, even on a Federation Priority One security channel.

Your commitment to Starfleet surely does not begin and end with the cloaking system. What would you say if I told you your device had disappeared?"

Flint replied, with a trace of irony, "That was, after all, the purpose it was designed for."

"No! I do not jest. I mean, it has been abducted."

"By whom?" Flint asked sharply.

"The details are sketchy, we still don't have all the facts . . . a skirmish on a small world . . . though some of us here at Starfleet are unwilling to rule out some kind of direct Romulan involvement . . ."

"You idiots," Flint said coldly. "Why was it not guarded properly? Why were precautions not taken?"

"It was being tested out in a small craft, and the craft was stolen. We don't even know if the thieves understood what they had aboard."

"And why was I not informed immediately?"

"The technology is ours now," the Tellarite said defensively. "And secrecy is of the greatest importance. We do not want our enemies to learn of the theft, or even to have solid proof of the device's existence."

"Well," Flint said, "I am sorry for you. I am sure it complicates your life. But if you think this news will tempt me to design new systems for Starfleet, you are mistaken. You have blueprints for my cloaking system and, as you say, the technology is yours now, and you can construct another if you wish. But consider this the end of my military contributions. I will design no weapons."

"Hypocrisy!" came the response, as the councilman's projected form buzzed and crackled. His image on the screen pointed its hard stump of a hand at Flint. "The cloaking device can also be an aid in battle. It can provide cover for one vessel attacking another. If you were willing to do that much for us, why will you not now come through with a weapons system?"

Flint stood before his screen and regarded him coolly. The sad eyes in the wise, noble old face stared into the fuzzy furious one of the Tellarite and found it difficult to understand. "The design problems involved in the cloaking device interested me. That is why I agreed to do it. But it is in essence a passive system, a means of escape from danger. I will design no aggressive systems, no new methods of destruction. And that is my final word."

"You moralize, and endanger the Federated Planets," the Tellarite sputtered. "The council is calling on you, in the name of decency, to help us, and yet you arrogantly shirk your duty, you turn your back—"

"Sir, I think you forget yourself," Flint said mildly.

The councilman stopped himself short, and recalled who this man was, in how high a regard the Terrans held him, and how beneficial he could be to the Federation. "My apologies, Mr. Flint." The words did not come easily to him. "We are all under stress at this time. I hope you will change your mind, and cooperate with the Federation in this matter."

"That is not at all likely. Please do not use the Priority One channel again for such a purpose."

The image of the Tellarite winked out. Flint walked away from the screen. He let his hand lean upon the curve of a marble statue, and sank against its coolness. He valued his hermitlike existence; exposure to such beings was most disquieting. Time had brought him detachment from passion; over the space of several millennia he had loved and fought and raged, and yet become ever more detached from the human drama, as repetitive blows and disappointments befell him.

Rayna had been his last emotional investment, and perhaps his greatest. Since her death, his fiasco with the officers of the starship *Enterprise,* and learning that he was soon to die, his detachment had become complete. How strange that these creatures could rage, could care about their petty threats and slights and rivalries and institutions, when all would crumble in a moment's time. For Flint there was only calm and quiet, the order that comes with knowing that all things are transient, ever changing. He had at last become a part of that flow. But what was it like to have such a disturbed, distorted spirit, to be as volatile, as suspicious as a Tellarite? What did it feel like?

Terror. Tunnel sight ahead to the screen, the ship's screen, and space was twisted, a tunnel sucking him in, and he gripped the seat to calm himself. Cold perspiration poured down his face. His fingers that had fired the phasers quivered in front of him. He stared at them, as if from far away. His ears rang, as if they still heard all the screams . . .

Jahn had to get control. Control of himself, but there was no control, he could not control the ship, nor Rhea, nor Pal, they were afraid of him, they saw him with a Grup's eyes, they saw him as a Grup, he saw the Grups coming, he saw the cities burn and everyone got sick and turned bad. He had flattened himself on the roof, near the chimney bricks, and watched and listened. *Then,* he was in control.

But now Pal was whimpering. Rhea was telling him hush. Jahn wanted to take care of them, *but they turn, they, the bitch, they both turn on me she won't let me near her, afraid of me,* and he couldn't talk good, was not in control. That one fact was clear. That was established.

119

He had been on the roof, and the Grups didn't get him, nyah, nyah, nyah, nyah, nyah, but then they got him, and it took them a very long time. Many centuries, they told him, when they came back. Onlies did not have time, but the Grups brought it back with them, with all their evil, and they seemed good, and *Miri, I'm sorry Miri and Miri believed in them and the Center came . . .* There were holes in his thoughts.

Voltmer Grup evil Voltmer hates me I've lost all control. Voltmer in the room with the chair I was on the roof the city burned they pushed me down I was on the roof and there were screams pushed me down the arm straps. And above my head . . .

Jahn got up and paced the cabin. Pal shrank from his movement, and Jahn felt like smacking him. "I'm going to lie down," he said, and his voice sounded strange. It was not his voice. "I'm going to lie down, Rhea, so you better take over. You're always saying I'm no good at maintaining the ship, anyhow."

"All right, Jahn. You rest."

Rhea's voice sounded too eager. Jahn eyed her suspiciously. "I'm going to sleep, Rhea. And you'll be running the ship. And you want to give it up to the Grups, suck up to the Grups, teacher's pet, that's what you want . . ."

"No, Jahn, don't worry, I promise I won't—"

"Well remember. Remember where we've just been. You heard people screaming in those alien ships. You remember the other ship? That was Federation. They tried to attack us—"

"No, they didn't, Jahn—"

"Quiet! They would have gotten us, and we killed them, crushed them. And now they're all after us. They'll take us back to Voltmer and he'll kill us and dissect us. So just think of that before you turn off the cloaking device. Think of that, think of that . . ." His scream had become one of hysteria, and he towered over her, felt he was viewing her from a great height, through a long tunnel. She blanched, and Pal huddled closer to her. Was that control? Was he in control? "I'm going, now," he said uncertainly, and fled through the swishing doors.

In the sleeping cabin he collapsed shudderingly, his head buried in a pillow. *Used to respect me I led the Onlies, me Dag Louise Miri I'm sorry Miri and I led them all the little Onlies and I was the greatest best and I could take care of them. Grups scared of me frightened the little ones Voltmer in my mind sucked me into tunnels. Wants to rule instead of me unman me I can't think good now. I can't lead. The lights were too bright the lights in the tunnel my hands strapped down there holes in my thoughts. My mind skips. I can't control, I'm sorry Miri, Rhea knows I'm not a leader now.*

He closed his eyes to block out the glaring white light that filled his mind. Thoughts flew in his mind like splinters of glass, like glass it hurt him to try to grasp on to them.

He had led. He had kept the Onlies, all there were, safe from animals, hunger, cold, and big Onlies who went bad. When the Grups came back it was hard for him. They would rule and he fought sometimes and Voltmer was scared of him, he knew it, *set out to destroy me, grow up, a lie, arms strapped down . . .*

They thought they could get him, but he'd kill them all, first. He could never go back, he had to get control, he'd show Rhea . . . In his mind he again saw the hull of the ships glowing, sending up sparks. *Blasts ripping into them, I'm sorry Miri.* Well, that just made it more final. Now Rhea knew they could not go back. If he rested, his mind would work good again. His thoughts would lose their walls, holes, tunnels, skipping, if he rested . . .

Jahn's form slowly relaxed into the softness of the bunk, and he drifted off into a nervous, much needed sleep.

Chapter Twelve

THE FEELING OF warmth and well-being that had followed Kirk for the few days he'd spent on Boaco Six had completely vanished by the time he stepped onto the bridge. The search to find the people who had beamed down for shore leave had been chaotic; they were scattered throughout the city of Boa. Two had been at a music festival, unable to hear the signal of their communicators. Kirk wanted them all beamed up fast, before the new hostility toward Starfleet among the Boacans got them into difficulty. One reported that he had already been threatened, goaded toward a fistfight.

Then had come the search for the members of the landing party; all were still in the bungalow except for McCoy and Rizzuto. They were spending the evening further pursuing their research. Kirk gathered his men and had them beam up directly—they could be debriefed at some later, calmer moment. Right now, he wanted facts.

"Scotty, what's been going on up here? Why wasn't I informed?"

Mr. Scott, with humility, sprang up out of the captain's chair, glad to relinquish it to Kirk. "I canna really say, Captain. Our sensors picked up readings of violence in space near this system's other populated planet. But I dinna think we should break orbit and investigate. I would have signaled you, but we were on the far side of the planet, blocked by the smallest moon when it happened. We'd only just come into communication range when you signaled for beam-up."

"Very good, Mr. Scott."

Lieutenant Uhura swiveled around on her chair. "Excuse me, Captain, but I intercepted a message in code from someone named Irina. She claimed that a ship from Boaco Eight had been destroyed . . . by a Federation ship!"

"So they've been telling me, Lieutenant. And I want to get to the bottom of this. Mr. Chekov, plot a course, at sub–light speed, to the scene of the attack. Tamara Angel thought this Irina's ship was done for—if we can save it, it will be proof of our goodwill."

"Course plotted and laid in, sir."

Kirk's palms flexed on the arms of his chair. All the lushness of that tropical world had not seemed truly natural to Kirk. *This* was his natural habitat. *Now* he was home. "All right, we'll be there in a few minutes. In the meantime, I want suggestions, possible explanations. Obviously, the Federation would not be out to attack a ship from either of these two planets. Well then, who would? Spock?"

The Vulcan had arrived on the bridge immediately after his captain and silently moved to his science panel. He cleared his throat. "Several possibilities present themselves, Captain. It could have been a Klingon ship disguised as one of Starfleet's. The Klingons would hope to aggravate the tension between the Boacan worlds, obviously, since they hope to spur the sixth planet on to go to war with its neighbor. The Romulans and the Orions also have a stake in the sale of weapons, and therefore in encouraging hostilities within this system. Indeed, for anyone who wants these worlds to go to war, and who wants Boaco Six to permanently distrust the Federation of Planets, such a terrorist act would be an excellent tactical maneuver."

Kirk nodded. "Well, we'll find out who it was. As soon as we see to this crippled ship."

The turbolift doors whooshed open and Leonard McCoy stepped out, already blustering before they had closed behind him. "Jim, you didn't have time to tell me in the transporter room. Well, maybe you can tell me now. What's going on? Why have y'all suddenly decided to pack up and come back on board? Do you know what I was observing out there? The inoculation programs that they've set up. Having children give each other shots and medicine, to increase their understanding and to minimize their fear. And then you take a notion that we just up and leave . . . ."

"Stand by, Bones. There may be wounded on the ship we're approaching. We may need you."

Spock walked over to McCoy and spoke to him quietly. "Sometimes, Doctor, your exuberance is less than beneficial. Understandably, you were reluctant to leave your fieldwork, and beam back aboard. But obviously the captain was facing an emergency, and valuable minutes were lost—"

"I came when I could, Spock," McCoy snapped. "I had my hand inside of somebody's gut, and I came when I could."

Kirk knew that there were times when the friendly bickering between the two took on a serious edge. Spock could not fully understand the doctor's uneasy relationship with Starfleet procedure and judged him harshly sometimes, though he respected his skills. And Spock's perfectionism and nit-picking only exasperated McCoy. As usual, the captain gently intervened.

"Tell me, Bones, have the Boacan patients who were on board all been beamed down? That's the important thing."

McCoy nodded. "Yes, yes, they're all back home. Some of them shouldn't be, weren't ready to be moved . . ."

"The Boacans made a special point of demanding it," Kirk said.

Helmsman Sulu slid his controls to slow the speed of the *Enterprise*. "Debris of the eighth planet's ship and the crippled sixth planet's ship appearing on the main screen, Captain."

It was a grim sight. The mangled scraps of one ship hung in space beside the blackened and battered hull of the second. The fact that Irina's ship seemed to be vaguely Romulan in its design did not lessen the grimness of its plight.

Spock spoke, bending over his panel. "It appears we are too late, Captain. No life readings from Irina's ship. It has apparently been flooded with poisonous gas, and the life-support systems, including temperature control, have been malfunctioning for over an hour."

Kirk pursed his lips.

Captain's Log, Supplemental:

It seems that we will have no survivors to present to the Council of Youngers of Boaco Six to regain their trust. Obviously, the one avenue open to us is to ascertain who is responsible for this attack and bring them to justice. I am still confident that it cannot be the Federation of Planets.

Lieutenant Uhura's hand moved to her earpiece to adjust the frequency of the signals she was receiving.

"Captain, it's Admiral Komack of Starfleet Command. Shall I put him on the main screen?"

"Yes, Lieutenant."

The dour, tired image of the admiral loomed above the bridge, wavering and crackling. Due to ion storms in this quadrant, communication with Starfleet was problematic, not always possible.

"Admiral."

Komack nodded shortly. "Kirk, you will abandon your current diplomatic mission to Boaco Six. If possible, you will resume it at a later juncture. But another issue of more immediate concern has arisen, and yours is the only starship in the area. There has been a small rebellion in a neighboring system, and a class five Starfleet vessel has been stolen by . . . marauders. It is armed and dangerous. An ore freighter has already been attacked, and we fear it may do more damage."

Though he had never really doubted it, Kirk felt relieved to see confirmed his faith that Starfleet Command had no knowledge of the attack on the two Boacan vessels. He opened his mouth to add to the admiral's information. "Admiral . . ."

"You've dealt with the problem of the system where the rebellion took place before, Kirk. So your experience may be of some use to you. The disturbance took place on Juram Five."

Kirk felt stunned. Old ghosts filled his mind. Juram Five. Juram . . . Five?

Chapter Thirteen

As Kirk took his seat, he surveyed the faces of those assembled around him in the briefing room. He did not show the deep agitation that he felt. Lieutenant Uhura had been called, and Dr. McCoy and Dr. Ramsey, a specialist in child behavior and child psychology. Kirk had left Scotty in command again, and Chekov and Sulu up on the bridge were making a sensor sweep of the quadrant, combing space for the renegade Starfleet ship. And Spock would be joining them in the briefing room shortly, as soon as Starfleet Command finished transmitting to him a more detailed report of the current situation. Everything that could be done was being done. Yet Kirk felt an exaggerated sense of impatience. What had happened? When they had last visited that system . . .

He called the meeting to order.

"Ladies and gentlemen, much of what we have to discuss here depends on the information that Mr. Spock will be bringing. But we can take this time to reassess what we already know.

"Juram Five is no ordinary planet. For centuries, it has had only a handful of inhabitants. The same inhabitants. Children who aged only a year with every passing century, who lived a wild existence, uninformed by adult discipline and understanding. Long ago, scientists on that world were experimenting with a youth serum, to lengthen the life spans of their people. What they came up with was a virus that spread like a plague. It prolongs childhood, but once the hormonal shifts that bring about adolescence and adulthood occur, the virus turns deadly. The entire population was swiftly contaminated, the adults reduced to brutal, raving creatures before they died. They took much of the planet with them in their final madness; destruction was massive.

"A handful of children were left alive, haunting a lone city, scrounging for food, living for centuries as a wild band, until puberty set in for them one by one, bringing madness and death."

Kirk paused, distracted by memories which had become raw and vivid in his mind. He was distracted mostly by concern for one particular individual. But he shook himself and pressed on.

"The *Enterprise* visited this planet on an early mission. We came into contact with . . . one of the children. We won her trust. Dr. McCoy was able to formulate a serum to counteract the effects of the virus—both the longevity it gives to childhood, and the degeneration that follows—and we left the children under the supervision of an emergency Starfleet team. And that is the last we have heard of them. Until now."

McCoy shifted in his seat.

"Yes, Doctor?"

"Captain, I'd just like to point out that the serum

formulated by Spock and me was not administered to all the children, just to Miri, and the others on the verge of puberty. And in the report I left behind for the Starfleet team, I recommended that the others *not* be decontaminated. I don't know if my recommendation was waived or not."

The doctor scratched his chin, trying to decide how to continue. At last, he said, "You know it's a question of ethics, a moral question, really, whether these children should be restored to a normal life span, or allowed to let the years before their adolescence spread over a millennium. Now, I wouldn't recommend infecting children all over the galaxy and distorting *their* lives that way . . . but, after all, in inoculating those younger "Onlies' . . ." McCoy glanced around. "The children called themselves the Onlies," he explained. "By inoculating those younger Onlies, we would be, in effect, *shortening* their life spans. And that is not exactly the usual practice of members of the medical profession."

"It's a tricky question, Bones. Childhood lasting for that long, centuries of immaturity—with adult supervisors constantly aging and dying all around you—could seem more of a nightmare than a blessing. And the comparatively short adulthood that followed seems a colossal cheat. Dr. Ramsey, could you fill us in on what was actually done with Miri and the rest of the Onlies?"

Ramsey was a young, thin, nervous man. A shock of white hair proved him to be an albino. He peered at the others through pink, blinking eyes.

"Yes, Captain. A very strange and interesting case, this. It appears that the team of specialists which took over after the departure of the *Enterprise,* after carefully weighing Dr. McCoy's recommendations, decided that all the children would benefit from being returned to a normal life span. Because they had been exposed to the virus for so long, it was necessary for the children to be inoculated repeatedly, on a regular basis. A school was set up on the planet to help the children to readjust, acclimate themselves to aging more rapidly, help them to understand its implications. And to 'civilize' them, or prepare them to become integrated with the modern galaxy, to respect adult authority, and so forth. From what I've read, the program was *not* an unqualified success."

"Have you ever visited it, Ramsey?"

"No, Captain. Only read about it in science digests. But I got the feeling the results of the program were mixed. It was run by a man named Voltmer. He's a somewhat controversial figure in the educational field . . . always urging a return to old-fashioned values and methods of teaching, with an emphasis on discipline, obedience, even learning by rote . . . it was felt by some that he was not the man for the job."

Kirk winced as he remembered the satisfied confidence with which he had left the world of Juram Five behind him. He had had no doubts that the team of specialists would help the children to readjust, give them the guidance they needed. . . . Federation experts in any field were, after all, only human—well, most of them. "What kind of problems were there, Ramsey?"

"Rebellion on the part of the children. Deep depression among some of the older ones. Distrust of their teachers, secretiveness. It appears these Onlies had developed a weird child-culture of their own during their years of isolation—that's what makes them so fascinating. Their own customs, almost a language of their own made up of childish gibberish, and remembered fragments of things from the adult world. Some of the children obstinately clung to it in the face of the changes they were going through. Or they'd fight for food, although it was readily available. Or they'd hoard it in closets and under beds. Or they'd refuse to wash."

Ramsey laughed nervously, and ran a wiry hand backward through his hair.

"Of course, many of the children adjusted beautifully. We had psychologists, anthropologists, and other researchers going in to test them a lot, though, trying to learn about the little community they had created for themselves before the memory of it vanished completely. Dr. Voltmer encouraged this—the children are such a curiosity, you see, their story has such interesting implications for a variety of scholars."

Kirk felt a wave of irritation pass through him at the stuffiness and insensitivity of the academic mind. He had seen the sad bizarre culture the Onlies had created for themselves amid the rubble of their world. He had borne the brunt of the anger and betrayal that they felt toward "Grups," as they called grown-ups, and had worked to restore their trust, and prepare them to receive adult care. For Kirk, Miri . . . and all of the children were not strange specimens, not guinea pigs for scientific research . . . the whole tone brought to this discussion was wrong!

He rose from his seat, paced the room rapidly.

"Well. It would seem that we have a pretty good idea of the causes of the trouble. Now, if we can only get the details—"

As if on cue, the doors slid open, and Spock entered, a tape in his hand. "I have the information here, Captain. Do you wish me to feed it through the

133

computer, or communicate the body of the report to you directly?"

"Blast the computer and all the red tape, Spock!" McCoy said. "Just tell us."

Kirk gave an affirmative nod.

Spock lowered himself into a chair, and steepled his long fingers before him.

"The Federation report is unclear on the exact sequence of events. But it appears that the causes of the disturbance were two of the older children. One was the boy Jahn, who in terms of physical aging is now nearly seventeen. The other was a girl named Rhea, who is now fourteen, in medical terms.

"Both children had proved apt students in some respects, and absorbed a great deal of information on the program. Rhea showed an aptitude for math and the applied sciences. Jahn was taken with engineering and spent a great deal of time learning about Starfleet, its procedures and protocol. Both were encouraged to pursue their interests, and made great use of the tapes in their school library. Yet both were also often discipline problems and proved most uncooperative in . . . tests they were asked to participate in.

"Apparently, these children, all the children, had developed with curious irregularity. Emotionally immature"—Spock seemed to use these words guardedly, grudgingly—"they had acquired surprising pockets of information from books, and experience over the centuries. At any rate, it seems it was possible for these two children to commandeer the class five vessel in question, a ship called the *Sparrow*."

Kirk swallowed. Hard. "So it was two of the children, then, who stole the craft. And who destroyed . . ."

Spock nodded. "It appears so, Captain. Who destroyed the two ships of the Boacan system. And severely crippled a Federation ore freighter, although its two pilots have survived." He seemed to hesitate for a second. "There is more, sir."

"Yes, Mr. Spock?"

"The vessel is meant to be manned by nine, but can be piloted by two, with difficulty. It was bringing dilithium crystals to resupply the power generators of the program complex, and most of the crew came planetside. The children were able to stow away, and then knock the rest of the crew out with sedatives, and beam them down.

"But apparently, Jahn decided to try to influence the other Onlies to come with them. He beamed back to the surface, to the children's recreation room, and was accosted by both security guards from the *Sparrow* and program staff, who tried to reason with him, to induce him to relinquish the ship. Several children became physically violent; Jahn was armed, and in the scuffle several of the adults and several of the children were killed. Rhea beamed Jahn back up to the ship, and a smaller child, a boy named Pal, physically nine years old, either went willingly or was abducted by them. It would seem that the violence and the killings utterly panicked the runaways, pushed them over the edge to complete instability. Hence their refusal to answer all hails and communication, and their completely unprovoked attacks on the ore freighter and the ships from the Boaco system."

As Spock paused, a heavy silence filled the room. He knew what his captain was thinking, what he would ask next. *If only I could tell Jim later, in private . . .*

"Mr. Spock," Kirk said quietly. "You say several of the children were killed in the skirmish on the planet. Did the report happen to mention—"

"It listed their names, Captain." Was there a gentleness moderating the Vulcan's speech? "Miri was one of them. She was killed by a stray phaser blast."

Captain James T. Kirk was no Vulcan. He felt it unhealthy, unnecessary to deny or suppress his emotional responses. He sank heavily back into his seat. The pain he was feeling flashed across his face for a moment.

But he *was* a commander. With responsibilities. Personal sorrows would have to wait. "You bring us harsh news, Mr. Spock. What a waste," he added, almost in a whisper. "Well! There still is that ship to be recovered." He flicked on the switch of the triangular viewscreen at the center of the briefing-room table. The face of Mr. Sulu, up on the bridge, filled the three screens.

"Any luck, Helmsman? Have you been able to track the *Sparrow?*"

Sulu's usually lighthearted face showed perplexity. "I'm not sure, sir."

"You're not sure? Either you have or you haven't," Kirk snapped. *Easy,* he told himself. *The pain is yours. Don't take it out on the crew.*

"Well, we've been getting traces of something, Captain. Could be a small ship. But they're occasional, spotty. They blink in and out. Appear and disappear all over the quadrant. If it's the same ship, it's following an awfully erratic course and traveling very fast. And ion storms simply don't account for the readings coming and going like this. Pavel says . . . that is, the only thing Chekov and I can figure is that they're using some kind of cloaking device."

136

Spock nodded. "I was getting to that, Captain. As you know, we have already penetrated the Romulan cloaking device, and so have the Romulans themselves; the technology in that field seems to have rendered itself obsolete. But the Federation, it appears, has been secretly experimenting with a *new* kind of cloaking device, which confuses, misinforms a ship's sensors rather than jamming them. The Flint device, as it is called, has proved most successful and difficult to thwart in tests. Too successful, perhaps."

"Flint device?" McCoy said, and frowned. "What's a name like that supposed to signify?"

Spock went on quickly. "What is relevant to our mission is that the *Sparrow* was equipped with just this device. Which is what makes the ship's recovery of even greater importance to the Federation. Its theft was a minor disaster."

Kirk moved to switch off the viewer. He said as he did so, "Mr. Sulu, continue your sweep. The next time you pick up sensor traces of the *Sparrow,* plot a course for it at maximum warp, and calculate as best you can its probable heading."

"Aye, aye, sir," Sulu said, and vanished from the screen.

Kirk felt very tired. *I like your name, Jim. I've sharpened some more pencils for you.* Killed by a stray phaser blast . . .

He shook himself. "Lieutenant Uhura. You were able to monitor the attack on the Boacan ships when the *Enterprise* was still orbiting Boaco Six. You intercepted Irina's message to the Council of Youngers. Was that all you picked up?"

"No, Captain. There were bits of . . . something else. It was fragmentary, crazy . . . I thought it might have been stray panicked signals from one of the ships under attack. Now, I think it must have been coming from the *Sparrow.*"

"What were these 'fragments' like, Lieutenant?"

"Gibberish. Phrases like 'Crush, crash, crush' and 'Police! Police under fire!' And 'See how bad, how bad, how bad I am.' Really strange to listen to."

Kirk thought of children in trouble. In so deep they knew they could never get out, could never go back. Who had done something too horrible to face up to with an adult's understanding.

He felt no anger at what had taken place. Only a feeling of sadness which swallowed him whole.

Chapter Fourteen

RHEA GAZED NERVOUSLY at the generator room's viewer, at the diagram of planets and constellations that glowed ghostly on its screen. She hit the border of the screen with impatience. She must chart a course for them to follow. They were going nowhere, going round and round. Even if she charted a new course, Jahn might ignore it, might refuse to lay it in. Jahn was acting crazy. Ever since they left Juram Five, the Home World. She still couldn't get Jahn to tell her what happened down there. Which of the Onlies had gotten hurt. If any of the teachers were in the slam-bang phaser show. Little Pal wouldn't really tell her about it, either. She wasn't so sure she wanted to know.

The fight with the big, slow, Federation cargo ship had taken her by surprise. She had stood still-rock, when Jahn opened fire, unable to grasp what was going on. And the destruction of the two primitive ships had been scary and awful. She couldn't talk to Jahn when he got like that, couldn't shake him from the ship's controls. He seemed crazy sure, and all she felt was confused. No matter what they did now, they couldn't make it better. So she had crouched down beside Jahn's swiveling seat, scrunched closed her eyes, and covered her ears with her hands. When she looked around again, the screen wasn't full of the disintegrating ships anymore; it was all stars again. The airwaves weren't full of the Grups' pleas and questions, the main cabin was silent. And Jahn no longer seemed certain, in control. He stared at her blankly, helplessly.

She did not know how to help him. They had planned the escape together, prepared for it, studied for it. But it had just seemed like a foolie, a game. Even when they were carrying it out, it was too easy, it didn't seem real. And now they couldn't go back. And she felt afraid of Jahn in lots of different ways. She didn't think she could do any of the things he might expect from her.

So when he looked at her that way, she had directed his attention back to the control panel. He was supposed to be the engineering expert, but he seemed to keep forgetting how to run the ship. She had to tell him again how to run the device that made the ship invisible—he kept forgetting all about it. She had seen little Pal curled up under a panel in the corner, whimpering, and reminded Jahn that they had to take care of him.

She had been a little Only, once. Then things had changed, fast, fast, fast! Grups had come back. The nice Grup man with yellow hair, and the devil, and the doctor. The pretty Grup lady. And Grups were good again, everyone said, they wouldn't hit and hurt. She couldn't remember that so well, the bad time, and the Grups that had belonged to her and gone bad, but the others did, some of them, but they said that these new Grups were all right.

And then came the Program. And the shots in your arm, that didn't hurt the way Onlies said shots in your arm hurt in the hospital foolie; but these shots felt funny, and you heard a hiss when the doctor injected you. And then time became fast. You felt more tired, more sleepy at night. You couldn't keep the new fancy clothes the Grups gave you—they got tight under your arms, at your waist; you had to keep getting bigger ones. The nurse would check you, see how you were growing, and then Dr. Voltmer and his esteemed colleagues would interview you . . .

Escape! Now that it had happened, there were some really good things about it. She liked the quiet on board the *Sparrow*. The darkened corners. After the bells and tones that punctuated the passage of time in the schoolroom and cafeteria, and the dorm. Onlies were smart. Onlies were feather-foot, Onlies could melt into a building or an alley when they wanted to. And that was what she and Jahn were doing now, melting away. The whole concept of the cloaking device appealed to her. It was Only-spirited.

Sometimes on the Program you could run and hide. But the Grups made you feel foolish. Took disciplinary action. "Go without dinner." Of course, an Only could go easily for a week hungry-belly, without food. But disciplinary action didn't feel good. And it was harder to go without food now that time was fast and her body was changing so fast. And thoughts changed; she changed, the way she felt about Jahn . . . no! Mustn't think about that. Change the subject. Think about . . .

When she was a little Only. That was nice. That wasn't bad. Then Jahn was always a lot older, a leader,

141

and he and Louise and Miri and also all those others who had gone bad and rotten, gotten the disease when they got too old, they took care of her and the rest of the little ones. Told you if you were being a bad citizen. Told you what Grups were like. Told you what foolies you were going to play.

Nothing made sense now. All her books and algebra and calculus could not make sense like a circle of Onlies, passing soup, or sharpening stick-knives out of old planks. Or a nestle of Onlies curled up for the night in a roof-cave.

They asked you how you felt. The Grup scientists. Them and their pills and things. They invented Grup evil long-ago. Miri had told her.

They'd put you in a white, white room, and there was just you, leaning back in the chair, there wasn't anyone else. They put phones on your ears and disappeared into another room with a big glass wall, except they could see you but you couldn't see them. They'd ask you questions. What was it like to be an Only? What was it like to live so long? How could you answer? It was what it was. How could you explain Onlies to a Grup? They made you feel little, they made you feel ashamed . . .

With their soapy water, and ear inspections. Shoes that pinched. Some were nice; Mrs. File was big and warm and shuffled about, and Rhea had built that small flying machine for her, spent all her free periods doing it, and when she turned it on and it flew around the classroom, and when she explained how she had built the gravity-antigravity component, Mrs. File had called her a very clever girl and given her a pretzel. In front of all the other Onlies. Mrs. File had a blue dress. And a red one with gold trim.

But what was bad, what was really bad was the

room with the chair. The lights were too bright. And Dr. Voltmer would turn on the bending noise, sonic waves it was called, and sometimes your mind would go a glaring white as the walls, you would go blank, you wouldn't know what you said. And sometimes he would ask you personal questions. Like, "How does it feel to suddenly be maturing at such an accelerated rate. Rhea? How are you coping?" Or he'd ask, did you feel anything about boys? What would you say to him? Tell him about when you and Jahn went walking down by the pool and you felt, no! Crazy, bad, a very bad citizen. Plot a course and we'll cut straight through the heart of the galaxy; they'll never catch us. Maybe if we stop getting the shots, we'll stop changing. We'll slow down and live like Onlies again. We don't need the Grups.

With the precise fingers of a skilled technician, Rhea plotted a course for the *Sparrow* to follow. It arced cleanly out of its original quadrant.

She did not know, nor would she have cared if she did, that it led into Klingon space.

Chapter Fifteen

KIRK LAY ON HIS BED, cool fingertips pressed against his
temples. Now that the search for the *Sparrow* was
under way, he knew he should give some thought to
Boaco Six and Boaco Eight and the strain on their
relations the children's attack on their ships had
caused. The death of the ministers had thrown relations between the two worlds into turmoil.

But his mind was filled only with memories of
Miri's planet. He reviewed over and over the series of
events that had taken place there. No . . . there was
no way he could have acted differently. They were
working so hard, so fast to cure the virus before it
killed them, *and* attempting to win the trust of the
children . . . There was no way that a different approach on his part would have made a damn bit of
difference. The mistakes, the difficulties in handling
the children came after the *Enterprise* had sailed on
toward her next mission.

He felt only pain, and a kind of regret, when he
thought of the peace and sense of well-being with

which he had withdrawn from the case, left it behind him. The children would be fine, he had thought; they're in capable hands; things can only get better for them. Perhaps he should have visited . . . but when, how? Too many missions, too many planets where he had left a piece of himself behind; were they all, thereafter, his responsibility?

Don't you know why you don't want to play the same games you used to, Miri? And why you don't see your friends the same way as you once did? It's because you're becoming a young woman . . .

All right, he shouldn't have left with such a feeling of complacency, should have been more aware that the bumps and jolts of the teenage years, as well as all the good things, lay before her and the others, in an even more concentrated form than for most youngsters. Oh, but *she* would have pulled through . . . He remembered Charlie X, the chance lost, but Miri had been saved, she would have been all right. Good God, the awful waste of it . . .

Kirk did not respond immediately when his door buzzer sounded. "Come," he sighed finally.

The doors flew open and McCoy stepped into the captain's cabin.

"Jim, Spock said you were off duty. But knowin' you, I figured you wouldn't be sleeping. Would you like me to give you a shot of something to help you rest?"

"No, that's all right, Bones." Kirk turned on the netted glittering sheen of the bed covers, lay on his back, and looked at the doctor through the half-light in which he had left his room. "Is it all coming back to you?" He smiled weakly. "Quite a mission, wasn't it?"

"Of course it's all coming back to me. But you've got to try not to think about it."

Kirk sat upright. "You know what must have happened? They've been mishandled because no one gave a damn about them. They weren't anybody's kids. No one could even identify with their strange situation. That's why they got turned over to some hacks."

"Well, Voltmer is respected by some. But *I've* never thought much of him," McCoy said drily. "But Jim! You've got to stop thinking about Miri, stop blaming yourself . . ."

Kirk sprang off the bed, a nervous mass, and moved to open the cabinet which held his Starfleet medals and decorations. "You know, she gave me something just before we left, as a . . . keepsake," he said, rummaging. "Here it is! Look." He held up in his hand a grubby, crudely carved wooden doll. At the sight of it, he could feel the back of his eyes sting with potential tears. He quickly replaced the doll in the cabinet and closed the door.

Spock's eyebrow shot up as his captain reentered the bridge. "Captain. You are surely not thinking of returning to duty?"

Kirk, with a jerk of his head, indicated that Spock should vacate the commander's chair and return to his science station. "Yes, Mr. Spock. Starfleet may send us an update on the Boacan situation, soon. And when we home in on the *Sparrow,* I want to make contact with the children. Under no circumstances can we fight them."

Spock remained firmly planted in the central chair. "It is unknown when contact will be made, Captain. You have only had five hours off duty, after a 14.26-hour shift. And according to regulations . . ."

"To hell with regulations, Spock!" Kirk felt a wave of impatience toward his implacable first officer, the bringer of bad tidings. "Return to your station. This is a mission I care about, and I'm supervising how it's carried out."

The Vulcan's expression remained impenetrable. In one fluid movement, he rose quickly out of the chair and glided up the few stairs to his science panel, relieving a frightened-looking crewman.

"Mr. Sulu," Kirk said tersely, "has the *Sparrow* made any more appearances?"

"Three, Captain. We've tried to use them to calculate its probable heading."

Chekov spoke. "Sir, it seems the wessel may have drifted into Klingon space, and drawn fire. This may have injured it—it seems to be traveling at a decelerated speed. And it appeared to be heading back in the direction of Juram Five. We're heading in that direction now, as well."

Kirk nodded approvingly. "Fine, Ensign. Let's hope they've decided to surrender the ship to the authorities of the Program. It would make life much simpler."

Lieutenant Uhura cleared her throat. "Sir, I'm receiving a signal from Admiral Komack again."

"Put him on the main screen, Lieutenant."

The familiar gloomy figure appeared, and Kirk swallowed his irritation at the meddling of the Starfleet paper-pushers in things they didn't understand.

"Kirk. You seem to be heading in the direction of Juram Five. The council feels it would be helpful if you locked into orbit there and learned more about the children from those running the Program."

"Captain!" Sulu interrupted. "I've got another

147

sighting of the *Sparrow* . . . it's heading away from
Juram Five, at warp two . . . we could easily overtake
them . . . no, it's gone, it's vanished again."

Kirk leapt up from his chair. "Plot most probable
course to intercept, Mr. Sulu."

The admiral spoke from the main screen. "Belay
that order, Mr. Sulu. Kirk, you are getting nowhere
chasing this ship all over the quadrant. You will
proceed to Juram Five and enter orbit there as ordered."

"Admiral, did you hear? The *Sparrow* is heading
away from the children's Home World. This is the
closest we've come to it. And it may be damaged, the
children may need immediate attention. Surely that is
of paramount importance. . . ."

"If the *Sparrow* is in real trouble, the cloaking
device will fail. Permanently. Meanwhile, it's crazy
for you to play cat and mouse with it all over the
galaxy. Proceed to your assigned destination."

The image of the admiral flickered and disappeared, giving way to a screen full of stars. Kirk
choked back frustration and rage.

Kirk, Spock, and McCoy waited silently in the
sterile, overstuffed lounge outside the office of Dr.
Voltmer on Juram Five. Pale Dr. Ramsey, the child
psychologist, stood examining a rather poor painting
of a supernova, done in lurid pastels, which hung on
the wall. He cracked his knuckles and hummed to
himself, behavior which put his captain very much on
edge.

All right, get a grip, Kirk told himself. He would not
let himself be overwhelmed by impatience to continue
the search for the *Sparrow*. There were useful things
which, perhaps, after all, could be learned here.

They had beamed down in the children's recreation room, in which Jahn's fight with the adults had taken place. All traces of the skirmish had been removed. They were met by Dr. Colignon, one of the staff, and escorted through long snaking white corridors, past empty classrooms of a dull metallic gray. Something should be done, Kirk thought, to brighten the facility. Nothing too elaborate or expensive. Some drawings by the children hanging on the walls would do the trick. But no indication of the children's presence could be seen or felt.

Kirk had brought Spock and McCoy along because he knew he was not at his best, and he trusted their counsel and judgment. And because they had been involved in this case from the beginning. And because he wanted to make it up to Spock for snapping at him. He hoped that his friend would understand that it was simply because of the strain he was under.

He needn't have worried. The Vulcan was far from feeling any hurt or resentment toward his captain. He was concerned about Kirk's health, because of the tension and stress he was suffering from, and his personal involvement with the mission.

There was something disturbingly obsessive about the way Kirk had pressed ahead with the search for the *Sparrow,* responding to every taunting glimpse of the children, against all odds of catching up with them. The captain took missions personally sometimes, if he felt responsible, blamed himself in some way for what had gone before. Kirk was not at fault, in no way culpable for what had happened on this world. But how to keep him from blaming himself?

Most of all, Spock was concerned because he had certain knowledge of *who* the man was who had developed the new cloaking device—the device that the *Sparrow* was armed with. The man who was perhaps the only person who could find a way to penetrate it. *If Flint is called in to help us,* Spock thought, *the strain on Jim will be even greater. And he won't be able to understand just why he is under more strain. He'll want to know. And it could open another old wound.*

Dr. Voltmer's doors glided open. He was a middle-aged, overweight, beaming man with a small nose and a pink face. "Gentlemen!" He shook their hands warmly. "So good of you to come. It's so terribly unfortunate, all of this. Yours is the starship that first made contact with the children, am I correct?"

Kirk nodded. "Mr. Spock, my first officer; Dr. McCoy, my chief surgeon; and myself were all on that mission. This is Dr. Ramsey, a child psychology specialist, from my ship."

"Ramsey! I read your article 'Rorschach Revisited.' Just wonderful work. I'd like to show you gentlemen around our center. The children are all taking naps during this period—"

"Dr. Voltmer," Kirk broke in sharply, "we're very much pressed for time. Our major concern at the moment is locating the small craft the children have taken. Once we make contact with them, we need to convince them to surrender the ship without a struggle. Any suggestions on how to do it?"

Voltmer lost some of his happy, easy attitude. "You may have troubles there, Captain Kirk. Very unstable youngsters. Violent and ungrateful. Rhea, the girl, has been a disciplinary problem in the past, though she seemed to be buckling down to work this past year—of course, she had unlimited access to Federation technical manuals." With an ironic laugh, he added, "We encouraged her interest." His face grew a darker shade of pink. "Now Jahn, the older boy, he's just a hopeless kid, bad through and through. He simply does not respond well to any kind of structured environment. He has challenged my authority, my role as director, on a number of occasions. He seems to think the center is his to run. He throws tantrums and, as you've seen, he's capable of anything."

The language, for an educator, was vindictive, unprofessional. The man must have a personal grudge against the boy; Kirk reasoned that this crisis could ultimately cost Voltmer his job. It would be no great loss.

"My advice to you," continued Voltmer, "is to take a firm stand. These children are very ambivalent in their attitude toward authority; they fight it and then they give way to it. Right now they must be feeling the lack of it. Rhea, at least, responds well to reason. Though she can turn quite uncooperative in certain areas of testing."

"What kind of testing puts her off?" McCoy asked.

Voltmer led them through a door into a white room, under glaring lights. A large white chair stood at the room's center. "Testing to augment her P.P.D.P., that is, her Personal Psychological Developmental Profile. And to augment our knowledge of the children's community, or lack thereof, before you rescued them."

"That chair . . ." Kirk said.

"Developed and used by Dr. Tristan Adams, at the Tantalus Colony," Voltmer said. "And abused by Dr. Adams, before he was debarred from practice and sent to a penal colony. Obviously it has been changed, adjusted, rendered harmless. We use it to calm hysterical patients, through sonic waves, and as much-modified aid to hypnosis. Through sonic suggestion, we help a patient overcome mental blocks, explore forgotten memories, memories sometimes centuries old, in the case of these children."

"Memories that they perhaps don't want to share with *you*," McCoy said gruffly. "If what you're doing is legal, it sounds pretty controversial, and not too far removed from what Dr. Adams used the chair for. It smacks of mind control."

"Hardly, Doctor," Voltmer said coldly. "And we do not believe in secretiveness and hiding things, here at the Children's Center. I stand by my work. I'm up for a citation for it. I take pride in it being 'controversial.' And it was you and your men, Captain, after all, who recommended discipline and close observation for these children."

Kirk stared at him, his face tight, disapproving. His communicator sounded. He snapped it open.

"Captain, this is Lieutenant Uhura. I am in contact with a Klingon commander, Commander Kreth. Aboard an empire battle cruiser."

Kirk frowned. Something new to juggle, another gambit being played, perhaps? "Where is he, Lieutenant?"

"The ship is within the parameters of Klingon space. But he is demanding audio-visual contact with you, and threatening to bring his ship into Federation space. What shall I tell him, sir?"

"Tell him to hold on, we're beaming up." He turned to Voltmer. "So sorry to run, Doctor. I'll give your suggestion about handling the children . . . all the consideration that it merits."

As the four Starfleet men stood together for the beam-up, Voltmer seemed anxious to regain a friendly atmosphere. "By the way, Captain, I'm told by one of my staff, Mrs. File, that you made a big impression on some of the children. Especially the girl Miri. She talked about you often, expected you to come back and see her. You were what I think we'd have to call her 'first crush.'" He chuckled, then, seeing Kirk's expression, recollected himself. "A real shame, that. A terrible tragedy. She was a fine little lady."

The landing party shimmered, dissolved away from his ingratiating words.

Back on the *Enterprise,* Kirk shrugged off the unpleasant mirth of the man he had left below. He stood before his command chair facing a new opponent.

The dark eyes of the Klingon Commander Kreth flashed. "So, you are the famous Captain Kirk. With all due respect, *Captain,* you can tell your authorities at Starfleet Command that this time they have overstepped themselves."

"What the devil are you talking about?"

"We in the Klingon Empire are not fools, Captain, and we are *not* to be trifled with. We protect our rights, *and* those of our friends."

"Get to the point."

Kreth drew himself up and paused dramatically. "Kirk, we are now on good trading terms with the planet of Boaco Six. And there is every reason to believe that this will blossom into an even *closer* relationship." He smiled, to reveal a set of gleaming white teeth. "And so we were dismayed to learn of the completely unprovoked Federation attack on a Boaco Six vessel, and another vessel from that system. The galaxy is seeing the true colors of the Federation with the destruction of these two helpless spacecrafts."

Kirk's response was crude, to the point, and a word not usually employed in the language of diplomacy. His crew on the bridge suppressed a collective laugh.

Kreth's eyes narrowed. "You may say so. But we believe that the *Enterprise* was involved in the attack, that the small vessel that perpetrated it was launched from *your* hangar deck. And that *same* small vessel recently violated Klingon space. It is responsible for the death of several thousand people, and property damage equivalent to the sum required to build a small space station. This time, Kirk, you have gone too far!"

"I don't believe you," Kirk said mildly. "The damage that ship did couldn't have been on anywhere near so large a scale."

"Quite unlikely, Captain," Spock affirmed from his station.

"You will, of course, repay the financial debt," Kreth continued, "but how can you make restitution for your other crimes? Your vicious insinuation to the Boacan ministers that *we* destroyed their ship . . ."

"It was one possibility we looked into. But that wasn't the case, and we admit it. The attacking vessel is of Federation make . . ."

"Aha!"

"But *not* under Federation orders. It was commandeered by several gifted but disturbed children who escaped from a children's center in this quadrant, who are behaving insanely . . ."

Kreth snickered. "Pirate *children*, you say? A very colorful excuse, Kirk, very creative, but not very plausible. No. These are clearly Federation terrorists, and you can never repay or live down the murders they have committed, the breaches of interstellar law."

"It's rather surprising," Kirk commented, "to see you becoming so adamant about space demarcation lines being respected. Considering the fuss your empire has been making about the Romulans' right to expand their space and their neutral zone in any direction they please."

"There is a subtle distinction between the two situations, Kirk," Kreth flared. "I am not surprised it escapes you, but I call your attention to it. The Romulans have not demanded the right to unloose spies and marauders across *their* boundary lines!"

"Nor has the Federation," Kirk countered firmly. "And that is why we intend to intercept and retire this small ship. You see, we *do* believe that space demarcation lines, recognized the galaxy over, are there to be respected and reinforced."

"Your actions show you think nothing of the kind. You have overstepped yourselves, and must be taught the consequences of such foolishness," Kreth menaced. "You seem to be simply asking for *war*." His mouth savored the word. He spoke with passion, and his eyes shone fiercely. "But you have not maneuvered wisely, Kirk. All your enemies are joining together against you."

"The Federation of Planets seeks always to avoid war. And it would hardly be to your interest . . ."

"You might like to know, Kirk, that the Romulan and Klingon empires are on closer terms now than at any time in the past. We were equally dismayed, you see, to learn that you have armed this renegade spacecraft with some sort of new cloaking device. And it will be in both our interests to put an end to such violent . . . experimentation, shall we say, on the part of the Federation."

"The day the Klingons and the Romulans trust each other enough to form a working alliance will be the day the galaxy freezes over," Kirk said with scorn.

Kreth again pretended that he had not heard. "And,

Captain, this is not the only friendship the Federation has cemented through its cruel and stupid acts." The Klingon visual transmission panned away from Kreth and revealed a figure standing beside his command chair. It was Iogan, the minister of public welfare from Boaco Six. There the boy was, making no attempt to hide the Klingon connection! Advertising it, rather than covering it up.

"You see, Captain Kirk," Iogan said, scowling, "Tamara Angel and I are sharing our duties, and jointly filling in for our lost comrade Irina. It is so very difficult to find a replacement."

"What are you doing on that ship, Iogan?" Kirk asked softly.

"The Federation has proven that it cannot be trusted."

"The Federation is your only hope of maintaining any control of that planet that you worked so hard to liberate."

"The Klingons have befriended the Council of Youngers . . ."

"I mean *real* control."

"Kirk," Kreth said, "you will confine your comments to the subject at hand and address them to me."

Kirk shook his head. "No. No, I'll address them to him, because he's still independent. You don't own him or his planet yet."

"This is not the time for Federation propaganda . . ."

"Take a good look around you," Kirk pressed on, directing his attention to the young minister. "Take a look at the ship you're on and how it runs. Take a good hard look at the Klingon Empire, at home and the far-flung planets that have come under its control. And ask yourself if that's the way that your planet should go. If the thousands who died in the struggle to liberate your world from the yoke of oppression, from rulers like Markor and Puil, if those thousands died to lead you to *this.*" Kirk saw Iogan blanch. "A puppet Klingon regime. Like it? Think!" he urged. "Think of who you're doing business with."

Kreth stepped in front of Iogan. "Kirk," the Klingon snapped. "I remind you again, you are pushing the united forces of the Klingon and Romulan empires to the brink of war. You can, possibly, prevent this catastrophe by reimbursing us for the damage done, and extraditing these terrorists of yours to the Klingons for trial and punishment."

"When the children are caught," Kirk said, "they'll be dealt with by our authorities."

Kreth's toothy sneer returned. "Dealt with, you say? Well, I hardly think, in light of the crimes committed, that a spanking will be sufficient. Think about what I have said to you, Captain." He inclined his head, still sneering, and the transmission of his image ceased suddenly, replaced by a soothing sea of stars. Kirk sank back into his command chair.

"Doubtless, Captain, the Klingons are communicating the same challenging message as the one Kreth delivered to us to Starfleet Command," Spock commented.

"Mmm," Kirk said. "They intend to milk this situation with the children's ship for all it's worth. They must know it's not really a spy ship."

Ensign Michaels, again on duty by the door of the turbolift, breached decorum in his anxiety. "Excuse me, sir. Do you really think they're going to declare war?"

Kirk waved his arm vaguely. "Not likely. The incident wasn't large enough, and I don't think they'd go out on a limb for the Boacans. Of course, relations have been strained for months, and this doesn't help any. It's the new cloaking device that's really got them worried."

"Ironic," Spock remarked, "seeing as the cloaking system was designed to be a deterrent."

"Didn't work out that way," Kirk said. "But I don't think even fears about that are enough to start a Klingon-Romulan alliance. They trust each other as little as they trust us."

Then Kirk thought of Iogan, and what his presence on the Klingon ship meant. Suddenly, he felt very tired. Perhaps he'd let McCoy give him one of those rest injections after all.

"Mr. Spock," he said, heading for the turbolift, "the bridge is yours."

Chapter Sixteen

TAMARA ANGEL stood gazing through a high stone window. Shafts of purple sunlight poured into the room, the rays playing upon her dark braided hair.

She was not looking forward to this meeting. It would be with someone she had met before, for preliminary talks; he had impressed her as slippery and evasive. He seemed to act independent of the wishes of his government. And he would have a further advantage now; he must know that her people were desperate.

Nevertheless, she straightened and turned with the pride of a strong soldier, as the timid rap played upon the battered door. A young girl's face appeared. "Tamara Angel, the representative of the Romulan Empire has just beamed down. He is waiting outside. But he has refused to let me take his weapon from him."

Tamara considered for a moment. "Do not press the point," she said at last. "Show him in."

The girl disappeared. She returned in a few moments, followed by a tall, swaggering Romulan. He stooped to pass through the low doorway of the small room used for one-on-one conferences. The pointed ears and ascending eyebrows, combined with a cruel sneer, lent him a very menacing aspect. His Romulan phaser was prominently strapped to his side. Tamara drew herself up to her full height; her glance let him know she was not impressed.

"It is good to see you again, Miss Angel," he said. "I hope that now we can clinch our deal."

"I am prepared to hear your terms, Agent Tarn," she replied.

"Very well. But there is little time to bargain. Your revolution must be helped quickly." The sympathy in his tone rang false, the voice was slippery, offensive. His manner contradicted everything Tamara had ever heard about Romulans. They were said to be a Spartan, reserved people, as befitted their Vulcan heritage. Though they had lost the fierce honesty of the Vulcans, and the strict code of logic and emotional repression, they were said to have retained Vulcan dignity. The first time she had met Tarn, she had expected the proud representative of a warrior race; she had encountered instead a conniving business-man.

"The Romulan Empire is at the service of the Council of Youngers," Tarn continued, "and our supplies can be delivered to you within the week. Let us finalize our agreement."

"I wish to know first," Tamara said, "in what capacity you represent the Romulan Empire."

"I am their agent in this exchange."

"And yet"—Tamara circled round him—"you are an independent arms dealer, are you not? The weapons and equipment we will be sent are largely of your procurement. And you will keep a large percentage of the profit."

"What is that to you?" Tarn's smile had vanished.

"I wish to understand the hierarchy of authority more clearly," Tamara pressed on. "If the equipment is inadequate, or if we are in any way dissatisfied, who can be held responsible? Do we appeal to the Romulan Empire? Or are we expected to try and exact justice from you?"

"The empire has authorized me to act, and will, of course, take responsibility for any difficulty I might cause," Tarn spat out. "Contact them, if you wish, and hear the promise from them."

"I *have* contacted them, several times," Tamara returned. "I have sent interspace coded signals asking this very question. But I still await their reply. The airwaves remain silent."

"Perhaps your signals never got through," Tarn suggested. "This quadrant is, after all, plagued by ion activity. Perhaps your transmitting equipment is of poor quality."

"That may well be," Tamara replied archly. "After all, it is of Romulan design."

Tarn shrugged. Tamara was infuriated by him, and by her position. Tarn was no fine specimen of a Romulan, but obviously, the empire had not cared to send one. The agent they had sent was a reflection of what they thought of her planet. Yet she and the council could not protest. The Orions could not supply them with the goods needed; the Romulans had the Council of Youngers, and they knew it.

"Very well, Tarn. Quote me your figures. How much can you deliver? And how much are you demanding in payment?"

Tarn gave her the figures, and when he quoted the

price her planet was expected to pay, she let out a shocked gasp, which dissolved into a laugh.

"You are joking, surely. The council could not come up with that sum in a year's time."

"That is unfortunate. But there are other ways you can pay. In argea, for example."

"Argea? What use would Romulans have for that? It is not a drug those with your physiology can use."

"No. But it can be refined, and sold to those who can use it through . . . unofficial channels." Tarn winked.

Tamara nodded. The Orions received argea payments for the same reason; to sell it on the black market to worlds with humanoid populations. Did the Romulans also engage in such traffic?

"Perhaps," Tarn went on, pushing recklessness over the edge, "it could be sold back to you. I understand your planet has a need of the drug argea."

Tamara counted to five, slowly. Her temper was checked. "In what form do you propose we deliver the argea?"

"We will send ships, to raze fifty miles of forest," Tarn said easily. "You may choose where on your planet it shall be. The ships are standing by to arrive tomorrow."

"You said delivery will not take place for a week," Tamara said sharply.

"Delivery must be made by a circuitous, unusual route. Surely you do not wish the Federation to know you are purchasing such a large supply of ships and guns from us."

"No. No, we do not."

"Nor your neighboring world, Boaco Eight. Best to keep the edge of surprise as far as they're concerned."

His left eye winked again. Tamara wondered, if he winked a third time, whether she would hit him.

"It is ridiculous to think we will let you rob our forests of so much argea, without our even having seen the shipment of materials you are sending. We have never before made so great a purchase from the Romulan Empire—"

"Have you ever been dissatisfied with our goods?"

"Often. But at least we knew we'd get them."

"I am insulted by what that implies, councilwoman. You had best not make enemies of us. If Boaco Eight declares war on you, what then, eh?" One of his slender eyebrows rose, to emphasize his point. "Will the *Federation* sell you arms? Better to accept our offer quickly."

Tamara swallowed. "Let us then, at least, scale down the deal." She tried not to sound like she was pleading. "The sea and air vehicles, the construction materials . . . let all that go. Only the spaceships and weapons are needed at this time."

"The size of the transaction was agreed upon last time," Tarn insisted, "and we are already at work filling your original order of goods. It is all or nothing. What is your reply? I grow impatient."

"I alone am not authorized to accept," Tamara lied. "The Council of Youngers will meet this afternoon and decide the matter then."

"I had heard that your council was in some . . . disarray?"

"That is not so," Tamara bridled. "It is true, we have lost an important, and much loved colleague." She fought the impulse to sink against the stone wall, stayed firm where she stood. "Another minister is away, others are on the opposite landmass. But those

163

who are here now will meet and decide on your *generous* offer."

"We await your decision," Tarn said with mock courtesy. "If I may be shown to my quarters, to rest . . ."

Tamara Angel called out to the girl guard who was waiting in the corridor, and she reappeared. She escorted Tarn out, and Tamara Angel kept her eyes locked fixedly on his back until it vanished. She was overwhelmed again by a feeling of injustice; the knowledge of how deserving, how unique, how important the people on her world were, and how little that meant in the larger scheme of the galaxy.

It was there Noro found her an hour later, sitting on the floor, immersed in the sunlight's shaft, her knees pulled up, her arms locked around the tops of her high boots.

"I was told you have called a council meeting," he said shyly. "It is about the deal with the Romulans, is it not?"

Tamara nodded. "They are offering us dangerous and unfair terms. I see no choice but to accept. But I think it should be discussed by the council, first."

"The council, such as it is," Noro said ruefully, with a ragged smile.

"There are enough of us here to discuss the issue," Tamara said, springing to her feet. "But I do wish Iogan was back from space, to be a part of this, to meet this Tarn. He who is always so keen on the Romulans, saying they can be trusted."

Noro ducked his head, tried not to look at how the sunlight caught her hair. His admiration of Tamara Angel was an old ache, an old friend, one he had learned to live with. It did not need voicing now, or ever. "Perhaps Iogan's trust is justified," he said. "Perhaps they are willing to invest in us as allies."

Tamara looked doubtful. "We are too unimportant for that, Noro. And too far away. I have a bad feeling about this," she added, thinking of Tarn's pointed ears and smirking face. "As if we are, as the humans say, compacting with the devil. Oh, these galactic arms dealers are all nothing but mercenary scum! Yet his government knows he is here. They chose him as their envoy. And there seems little alternative—let this be a test, then, of Romulan friendship and respect."

They had left the small conference room and headed out into the corridor. Noro told her of progress at an education center on the other landmass. Tamara listened, but her mind wandered back to thoughts of Romulan cargo ships, shooting through space at a dizzying speed, loaded with . . . new strength for the revolution? Could it be true?

She had traveled the stars once, in such a ship. In the days of Puil, she had been sent to school and university on Federation Planets, had absorbed their ways, their style of dress, had returned to take her place among her planet's elite . . . and then turned her back on all of that. She chose to discover, instead, her world and its people.

"I have heard from my little brother," she told Noro. "He visited me last night. I think my parents know he sees me, and he says they are learning to live with the times. Peace talks between us may soon be possible." She laughed.

"That in itself is encouraging in such violent times," Noro said. He had never left Boaco Six; a breathtaking trip to one of its moons as a child was the farthest he had ever been. He was a fearless fighter in battle, and a good minister—social skills he had none. He always simply stared at Tamara with a kind of comical awe. She felt a wave of affection for him and squeezed his hand.

"Come, my old friend," she said. "It is time for the meeting of the council. The others must have gathered by now."

"Will you put it to a vote?"

"Yes. I will tell them Tarn's offer. And we will vote."

Noro followed her through the echoing hall, to the doors of the great chamber. Tamara's thoughts were again of space, and wondering if all that cold vastness contained a single friend. If so, where was he now?

Chapter Seventeen

Captain's Log, Stardate 6118.9:

Our attempts to locate the crippled *Sparrow* have been unsuccessful. Helm reports that an unusual number of small ion disturbances in space are impending the search. The Klingons are becoming more belligerent, and Starfleet has informed me that the planets Boaco Six and Boaco Eight may be preparing for a civil war within their solar system. Klingon and Romulan arms are being delivered to Boaco Six at an increasing rate, according to intelligence reports. If war breaks out, the Federation will have no choice but to arm the other side.

Time is running out. Starfleet is calling upon Flint, the man who invented the new, experimental cloaking device, to help us penetrate and recover it. Mr. Flint is, of course, the great ancient creative genius, the Methuselah who has lived through most of Terran history, and given us so much. Calling on him for help seems a wise move . . .

Yet I am troubled by personal concerns. Something gnaws at me which I cannot define. I believe I have come to terms with Miri's death, and the catastrophe of the Onlies. Thanks to my chief surgeon's injections, I am better rested. What is it, then, that makes me so uneasy?

* * *

KIRK WONDERED when he would again feel at peace with himself. Ever since the order had come from Starfleet Command to enlist Flint in the search effort, Kirk had felt restless; voices and nameless shadows kept appearing and fading in his dreams, and disrupting his thoughts as he sat in his command chair, or alone in contemplation. His dreams were violent and strange. He would awake periodically in a nervous sweat, searching for a clue to their meaning, then drift off again, letting them envelop him.

He could remember little about his earlier encounter with Flint—which was odd. He had a good memory for the people and events woven into his life throughout his space travels. Yet his recollections of Flint were vague and blurry. Such an impressive individual, who had given so much to human culture, would surely have had a lasting impact on one's mind. Kirk could conjure up his face, but nothing of their conversations. What he felt toward Flint was violent emotional rage, bitterness, and embarrassment . . . how could these feelings have been caused by this miraculous man? Kirk could not account for them. It puzzled him greatly. The answer seemed always in reach, always eluding him. Even in dreams.

It was a quiet day in sickbay. A few crewmen had come in for checkups, a young lieutenant rested on warmth pads to heal a shoulder muscle she had strained in the gym. Leonard McCoy had left Nurse Chapel in charge, had spent most of the day scanning tapes on the situation of the Onlies and the program that had been set up for them, and then tapes of Flint's accomplishments since he had been discovered and identified by the men of the *Enterprise*. The list was impressive: contributions to the arts and music, to medicine and physics. But McCoy was worried about the captain. *Why Flint? A thousand inventors in the galaxy . . . why did he have to be the one pioneering the new cloaking device?*

McCoy pulled the tape he had been viewing out of the computer and threw it down on his office desk.

"Christine," he said, as he ambled out the sickbay door, "I'm heading out for some lunch, be back in an hour or so. Keep an eye on things, will you?"

"Certainly, Doctor," Nurse Chapel assented.

McCoy soon found himself in the major mess hall of deck five, hit by a dizzying array of aromas. A food computer programmed with two hundred thousand recipes made every cafeteria on the *Enterprise* smell like a smorgasbord. But McCoy knew just what he wanted.

His fried chicken seemed to sizzle and crackle up from the plate in front of him, as he plunked himself down at an empty table. A few feet away, Helmsman Sulu was explaining the finer points of fencing to an admiring crowd of friends. But McCoy felt in no mood to socialize with the crew. *Jim has enough on his mind, what with Miri's death, and what's happened with the Onlies, and this whole damn Boacan entanglement. Why did he need to be reminded of Rayna?*

The beautiful and brilliant robot girl, Flint's creation, had fallen in love with the captain, and he with her. Discovering that she was an artificial construct did not lessen Kirk's love for her; he declared she had *become* human. Kirk and Flint had fought each other, recklessly, madly, for Rayna. She was overwhelmed by having to choose between the two of them, by the pain she was causing both of them, and short-circuited, died . . . however you described it, it came to the same thing. The ancient Flint and the young

Kirk had been heartbroken, abashed . . . hardly an experience that either would want to be reminded of. Especially now, this way.

And it was painful for McCoy to be reminded of it. He had felt for the captain's grief, and had lashed out, perhaps unjustly, at Spock. The Vulcan seemed too cryptic, too aloof, to deal with at such a time. McCoy told Spock that he felt sorrier for Spock than for the captain. Because Spock would never know what love could drive a man to. The glorious victories. The glorious defeats. He had left Spock deep in thought as Kirk slept finally, slumped over his desk. They had never again discussed the matter.

No emotions . . . Well, it must simplify things for him, in the long run. By suppressing his human half, Spock seemed to think he gained something, achieved something.

McCoy picked up a piece of chicken and took a halfhearted nibble; the flavor revived his spirits somewhat. He'd be glad when this whole cloaking-device caper was over, and he could go back to his research on Boaco Six. Those crazy young ministers and health workers . . . he'd found that world stimulating and refreshing. And it would be good for the captain too.

From across the mess hall, Spock watched him. McCoy did not notice him as he headed for the food dispenser, then hesitated for a moment. At last he moved soundlessly across the room until he stood beside McCoy, and made him jump when he spoke.

"If I might have a word with you, Doctor." He slid onto the bench, placing his tray on the table. McCoy surveyed his food selections; Spock had a Vulcan *torbak* salad, a tall glass of water, and what appeared to be an Earth dish of broccoli mixed with snow peas, Asian in origin. A meal ascetic enough for any monk.

Damn that pointy-eared Vulcan! McCoy had been looking forward all day to tearing into some juicy home-style southern fried chicken, but the vegetarian science officer always made him feel self-conscious about enjoying meat. He took another cautious nibble.

Spock seemed to sense his uneasiness. "Do not let my eating habits trouble you, Doctor. I long ago ceased to wonder how a healer of human flesh can take pleasure in the cooking and eating of other animals. Please continue to enjoy your meal."

"Thanks a lot," McCoy grumbled. He laid down his food and looked at Spock. "What was it you wanted to talk to me about?"

Spock spoke quietly but earnestly. "As we will soon be approaching Flint's planet, and as you are the only other person who is aware of what happened during our previous visit there, who knows what our experiences were . . . it is necessary for me to tell you that the captain no longer remembers them."

McCoy responded with the violent emotional reaction which Spock feared this news would excite.

"What do you mean he no longer remembers them? That's impossible! I admit, he stopped speaking of the fight with Flint, and of Rayna pretty suddenly . . . I was glad he put it all behind him . . . just what have you been up to, Spock?"

Spock, in a rather un-Vulcan gesture, pushed the blue *torbak* salad aimlessly about on his plate. Perfectly vile-looking vegetable, to McCoy's way of thinking.

Finally, Spock spoke. "I used the Vulcan mind-meld to help the captain forget. It was necessary that he put the experience behind him. So that he could command more efficiently."

McCoy was touched. The mind-meld, he knew,

involved a degree of mental intimacy, a loss of privacy which Vulcans found most distasteful, and avoided whenever possible. "I guess I was a bit rough on you that night, Spock. Said some things I shouldn't have. What . . . made you do that for Jim?"

The Vulcan remained impassive.

"Well, anyhow," the doctor said, "since you say he doesn't know about it, I won't give you away. Things could get complicated, though, when Flint comes on board. He may want to talk about Rayna, about the whole episode."

Spock nodded. "A possibility I have considered, Doctor. However, it seems more likely that Mr. Flint will wish to avoid all discussion of the past, and concentrate on penetrating the cloaking device he designed. Let us handle each contingency as it arises. But I believe, for now, it is best to leave things as they are."

Flint lay before a crackling hearth of sweet-smelling wood and rosy fire. His fingers dug into the deep harsh wool of his fine exotic rug. He idly traced the pattern of a vine stem as it snaked around another, with his fingers. His thick eyebrows, his sad stern features were immobile.

Flint, the man who had been Methuselah, Solomon, Alexander, Merlin, Brahms, Leonardo . . . Flint, with no project at hand, no diversion, could at last feel his rugged old leathery body aging. It was a strange thing to feel.

Of course, he had aged up to a point, millennia earlier. He had started his life in 3000 B.C., in Mesopotamia. He was Akarin then, a mercenary soldier, a bully, and a drunken fool. He grew from boyhood as Akarin, and was pierced to the heart in battle. When he did not die, he became aware of the strange gift that he possessed, the gift of rapid tissue regeneration. Veritable immortality. His aging process slowed, and halted when he entered a virile early middle-age. It was then that he had to undertake the business of his life; traveling from place to place, hiding his true nature by moving on before others could remark it. His dazzling wealth—his private planet had been bought with a modest fraction of it—and his equally dazzling store of information and wisdom had come with centuries of acquisition. Yet wisdom and wealth could not assuage the most unlikely characteristic of immortality: an ennui that could paralyze him, make it all seem worthless.

A hundred different professions. Languages. He would learn new ones to amuse himself. Years of travel and carousing would give way to centuries of longing for security, for one precious, lasting love. And in those centuries came girl after precious radiant girl, clutched to him until she withered, turned to dust. Cynical years of carousing and numbness would then follow, a resolve to never love and mourn again. And then . . . he would trip again, be pricked again by a loveliness so startling, a girl he cherished so deeply that he knew they could never be sundered . . . until the woman withered, turned to dust.

Twice he had tried to follow them by taking his own life. He hanged himself in Cadiz in 712. The rope was cut by his interfering, swart, stupid landlady. His unconscious form was lowered, and soon he breathed life again; dead tissue gave way to living.

In 1419 he lost Chloe in a village in Bordeaux. He was playing the part of a wealthy baron at the time, had a house well-run with serfs, servants, and courtiers. He shut them all out after Chloe's burial, pictured

173

her honey hair, heard her voice calling him, took a
knife from the wall and cut and slashed his chest,
goring and carving several vital organs. Unconscious-
ness engulfed him. He did not truly expect to die. But
it amused him to lie in bed during the weeks that
followed, feeling his body renew itself, a film of new
flesh forming over the healing organs, the sting of pain
distracting him from a deeper wound, his recent loss,
and masking the dull, aching, ever-present lack of
some sweet constant in his life. Scars remained, after
his body healed, for several decades. Then they, too,
melted away.

But this flesh-carving proved to be frivolous; a
servant had spied on his convalescence, and spread
stories of witchcraft and forces of the occult at work in
his manor. It forced Flint to flee, to Italy this time . . .

All the dates and wars, brides, achievements, places
. . . sound and fury, signifying nothing. Incidents that
stood out in his mind, centuries that sped up to a blur,
undistinguished, unremembered. What soured Flint
on so many women and so many bosom friends was
an inescapable feeling of contempt. An impatience
with their blearing eyes, wandering minds, creasing
faces, trembling hands growing ever feebler . . . And a
feeling of rage, almost jealousy, that their short spans
made their lives sweeter, seemed to give them meaning. They could choose some quaint little toy village
in which to live out their days, and have it be their
world. They would never return to see it portioned
into pastures for the rich, burned, sacked, or paved, or
renamed, its monuments and houses of worship razed
and replaced, or its industries mechanized, or the
streets giving way to malls and lots, or the air jets of a
city in the sky . . . Flint had watched the human
circus on parade going by, had at times contributed to

it, or manipulated it, until at last, disgusted, he retreated into solitude. Yet his friends, his loves, the rest of humanity knew only the bliss of mortal ignorance.

And I am mortal now. Flint rotated his ankle experimentally. It twinged sharply. Something wondrous and new; even the ankle seemed surprised. Arthritis had been appearing for a month, steadily insinuating its way into his muscle joints and limbs. "The thrill of deterioration!" Flint said, and laughed. "We see now the meaning it adds." He had talked to himself when alone, as to one trusted companion, since before he left the Valley of the Euphrates and Southwest Asia and embarked on all his travels. When he fell in love, or had a family, he tended to lose the habit. Since the death of Rayna, he had begun talking to himself once again.

Rayna . . . sweet mortal twinge for the two of them, meant to have been immortal. Rayna, his Pygmalion's creation, the culmination, synthesis, orchestration of his love and all his most cherished dreams. Dreams nurtured, with her near him, for a handful of decades. Rayna, his child, student, protected one, his mother, sister, lover, friend, female companion for all time . . . but the story had never been completed. She had never found maturity, or her capacity to be completely human and love as a woman, until too soon, too late, too suddenly.

Did he hate the impudent young captain whom he had used as a puppet, his pawn, his initiator? There was no hatred in him, not even a bitterness left. Flint had acted as foolishly as Kirk, after all, for all his age—and now he was as mortal.

Rayna's death, Dr. McCoy's discovery that Flint, away from the elements and atmosphere of Earth, was

175

slowly dying, and the departure of the men of the *Enterprise,* had left Flint with a curious sense of peace. Perhaps the peace he would have felt had Rayna lived and learned to love him—perhaps sadder. But a peace that gave him focus and set him working again, with a deadline at last. No longer did he merely dabble in long-neglected music, painting, and experiments. He set aside time each day for each. Yet, he rushed nothing. Every moment, active or idle, was sweeter, and he savored it. Such pleasure, in lying alone before a magnificent smoky blaze that stung his eyes with water. *Man's greatest achievement, capturing fire, came long before my time. We are foolish to think we have outgrown it.*

A metal whirr filled the room. The loyal machine hung in the air by the old-fashioned door of Flint's study. It moved toward him, gliding through space, the firelight shining off its curves and angles with a steely glint. He absently admired the new, modified robot servant, designed to meet his current needs. He had added the voice component to it for the mild diversion of having someone else to talk to now and then. Its new metal arms hung limp for the moment. It stopped in the air near Flint, and hovered, suspended by its antigravity unit.

"Yes, M-7, what is it?" Flint asked.

"Signor," the robot whirred, "the dilithium splinters have been prepared, as you requested, for the cloaking experiment."

"Very good, M-7," Flint answered, easing to his feet before the robot could offer to assist him. "Let's get some work accomplished before the Earthmen arrive and want results."

The device he had designed had been stolen and misused, and he wished to participate in its recovery.

So he would sacrifice his privacy, would mingle with ordinary people again. The thing he had said he would never do. He had finally consented to Federation requests that he join in the search for the *Sparrow*. He viewed the future with reservations, especially about the starship he would be boarding—but also with a touch of excitement. Could it be that he still missed the society of others?

He moved gingerly through the door, bemused by the pain in his right leg. The robot lingered, to spray the fire in the hearth with a water mist. The flames hissed and died. M-7 followed Flint to the laboratory.

Chapter Eighteen

KIRK HAD ORDERED his officers to turn out in full-dress uniform when Flint was received aboard the *Enterprise*. A tape of "Variations for a String Quartet in Dm" recently composed by Flint was playing in the transporter room and throughout the ship as he was welcomed aboard and courtesies were exchanged. Starfleet and the Federation of Planets recognized this exceptional man for who he was, and who he had been, and had decorated him many times over in recent years for his services to humanity, though he had refused to attend the ceremonies. Now that he had been lured off his private planet to help search for the *Sparrow,* Starfleet Command had urged Kirk to fete him, shower him with honors.

Kirk knew the measure of the greatness of the man, and agreed he should be honored. He would do all that was appropriate. But what was this feeling of *repugnance* then, when Flint's form shimmered into existence on the transporter pad, and his robot servant materialized, floating behind him? Why did Kirk distrust them both, want to challenge Flint, accuse him . . . of what?

Still, knowing what his job required, Kirk managed to force a smile, stepped forward, and bowed. "Mr. Flint, our ship is graced by your presence. It is regrettable that we meet again under such trying circumstances. We will do everything possible to accommodate you."

Flint stepped off the transporter pad and moved toward Kirk, studying his face, surprised by such a genial greeting, wondering if it was meant as irony. "I hope my efforts will be of assistance in tracking the missing ship," he said at last.

"Starfleet has every confidence in you," Kirk said, still with forced amiability. He suppressed an irrational impulse to pull back and punch his august guest right in the jaw. *What's wrong with me? I must be becoming unhinged.*

McCoy stood to the side, at attention, his mouth in a sardonic smile as he watched the exchange. Spock observed it with his brows furrowed in a frown of concentration.

"You remember, of course," Kirk continued, "these two gentlemen, Dr. McCoy and First Officer Spock."

They bowed in Flint's direction.

Flint nodded toward them. *Is Kirk trying to shame me with his nonchalance, his forgiving behavior? Or did my Rayna mean so little to such a busy young man with so many romantic intrigues behind him?* "I am anxious, Captain, to begin work on penetrating my cloaking device. If you would be good enough to show me to my quarters and the laboratory facilities at my disposal . . ."

"Certainly, sir. Mr. Spock will conduct you to them."

"If you will follow me, Mr. Flint . . ." Spock said, anxious to end this interview, moving toward the door.

Flint paused. "There is some equipment I need, still on the planet. M-7 will see to its transport." The robot moved to the transporter consul beside Mr. Scott, who looked dramatically formal in his kilt-styled dress uniform. M-7 inched him out of the way and began punching in coordinates and pulling levers with its long mechanical arms.

It didn't have arms! Kirk thought, glad of a certainty about the past. This must be a new model. "Once you're settled in, Mr. Flint, I'll send technicians to assist you in your work." He was glad to at last see the doors whoosh shut on Spock and Flint, and gave a violent shudder of relief.

Spock watched Flint come on board with what a human would have called a feeling of pain. Obviously, he told himself, he could not have foreseen this. The odds against the ship-obsessed career officer Kirk, and Flint, the avowed recluse, being brought together again on a mission were quite astronomical. Logically, it would have been foolhardy to even consider the possibility. As if he had been attacked, questioned, pressed for it, Spock made the calculation in his head. Odds of easily 6,248.3 to one.

He could hear, in his mind, the voice of McCoy, mocking him. "For all your roots and percentages, Spock, you sure don't know much about life. Life is capricious, and it doesn't perform according to your tabulations." As usual, Jim had beaten the odds. But this time, the situation in which he'd done it was a disaster.

Entering Kirk's mind that way had not been a

regulation move, but this did not concern Spock. He would gladly face court-martial, or give up his life if it meant helping his captain. But *had* he helped him? If he was hurt in the days ahead, the fault would belong to no one but Spock, and his miscalculation.

He led Flint to a small laboratory adjoining engineering, in which Flint could conduct his experiments. Spock explained some of the intricacies of the current computer system, and Flint inserted a tape of information into its consul. Soon he was viewing blueprints and graphs on the room's main screen. The Vulcan stood by him, watching. Occasionally, not looking up, Flint fired questions at him.

"Mr. Spock, I am looking for a flaw in my device. I do not expect to find one, but I am looking. You say the children's ship exposed itself at intervals, then disappeared again. Were the intervals at all regular?"

Spock had no clues to offer. "No, sir. Our helmsmen tried to calculate this, to plot it on a graph in time and space. Their findings show that there is no discernible pattern to the *Sparrow*'s appearances. How often they occur, the light-year interims between them, the speed of the craft, all seem to be erratic, entirely random. This leads us to believe that the children occasionally switch off the device, or do not take the proper steps to maintain it. In the same way, they have occasionally used ship-to-ship radio—perhaps to taunt us."

Flint nodded.

"Of course," Spock went on, "these calculations were done before the *Sparrow*'s incursion into Klingon space. Their warp drive seems to be gone, now, and Starfleet has assured us that the other ship systems will soon be going critical as well."

"Did they?" Flint said. "Unfortunately, Starfleet Command really knows nothing of my device. In a ship altered for the use of my cloaking device, the device will be self-protecting. It will maintain itself at all costs and, in a crisis, divert power from other failing systems for its own needs. It considers itself more important than warp drive, phaser power, even life support. It was designed to provide last minute camouflage in a danger zone, a combat situation. Only when the sentient beings aboard are lethally threatened by heat and oxygen loss will it give another system priority over itself."

Spock considered the complications this presented. "A system as hardy and enduring as yourself, sir," he said. In the past, he and his captain had encountered other such obsessive geniuses who tended to design their computers and machines in their own image.

"As hardy and enduring as I *once* was, Mr. Spock, before I chose to wander into space, away from Earth. I have proved vulnerable—so must my device."

He returned to his charts and calculations, tested a thousand times before for accuracy, hopefully probed now for a sign of weakness.

Spock watched him but did not speak again. Flint soon began to mutter to himself; Spock's excellent ears were able to pick up remarks about personal folly, how a defensive weapon had become the cause for galactic confrontation, he never should have designed it . . . Spock realized Flint was simply talking to himself. Perhaps he had forgotten Spock's presence entirely.

The murmurings died away, as Flint seemed to have hit upon something. He was asking the computer for readings of various substances, their chemical make-up, and the feasibility of reducing them to powder.

After two hours had rolled by, Spock ventured to remark on this—his curiosity was tugging at him.

"Mr. Flint, if I may venture an observation, the methods you are using, the experiments you are conducting, have little to do with cloaking device technology, as I understand it."

Flint nodded. "Quite correct, Mr. Spock. And that is because the cloaking system I developed was a major break from the usual methods of cloaking a vessel, hiding it from sensors. Earlier, more primitive devices sought only to *mask* a ship. Mine confuses sensors so that they pick up unclear or completely false readings. They will report that the ship is in several places at once. Or they report it to be an asteroid, or a pocket of asteroid rubble. Or they read it as an ion storm, a quite effective illusion in this quadrant. Or they sometimes read it as the empty void of space. The device causes the illusions to alternate and provide the ship chameleonlike camouflage which complements the ship's surroundings. For example, it will read as an ion storm in an area where real storms frequently occur. The illusion of the void of space is the easiest to penetrate once the ship is generally located. But it will never maintain that illusion for too long."

Spock nodded, impressed. He had not understood before precisely what was meant when Starfleet's secret tapes stated that the Flint device "misinformed" sensors. "A most clever method to use, sir."

Flint smiled. "Too clever, I'm afraid. I tried to invent a cloaking device that could not be penetrated. I may have outwitted myself in the process."

"Then you see no hope?"

"Not of getting clear sensor readings of the *Sparrow*, no. You see, even if we penetrate several of the illusions, the device will have many more still in store, and it could, if necessary, project an illusion far away from us, as a decoy, to distract us ... What I am pursuing now is the idea of throwing some substance at the ship which will stick to it, make its outline discernible. The substance must adhere to the hull of the ship, must be producible in mass quantities, and, as it coats the *Sparrow,* be beyond the cloaking device's ability to hide it."

"Of course," Spock said, on his face a look akin to excitement. "Yet you've been experimenting with granulated trititanium, and dilithium splinters ... the *Enterprise* cannot produce these in large enough amounts ..."

"I am aware of that, Mr. Spock. So, something cheaper is needed, something producible in bulk, but with the same qualities as these substances."

"Properties of both energy and matter?"

"Exactly," Flint said.

"Mmmm," Spock fairly purred. "I shall instruct engineering to take inventory of all such substances on board, and to supply you with a list."

"That would be most helpful."

Silence fell again as Flint monitored on his computer screen experiments with antimatter being conducted in a decompression chamber on the other side of the ship. The antimatter proved too volatile and unpredictable to be useful. "As I expected," Flint said softly. He punched the results into the computer's problem-solver information bank. "Mr. Spock," he said mildly, as the results of the experiment were tabulated, and another trial substance was selected by the machine, "your captain, to all appearances, harbors no ill feeling toward me. Is this, in fact, the case?"

Spock hesitated, then replied, in a voice impossible to read. "It is unknown to me precisely how the captain now regards you. Or what his feelings are about what occurred when we visited your planet."

"And yet his duty to Starfleet, and to me as a guest, appears to be his first consideration. Such strength of character in a man is to be admired."

Inwardly, Spock firmly agreed with this view of Kirk. But he wasn't sure that it was this, exactly, that had motivated him to be so genial to Flint in the transporter room. He was eager to redirect the conversation and had been curious about Flint's behavior since the remarkable ancient had come on board. "If I may venture to say so, sir, *your* bearing and behavior seem changed from what they were when we were on your planet. You seem at peace . . . somehow more calm and resolute."

Flint smiled slightly. "Yes, Mr. Spock. Grief over Rayna's death, and knowledge of my new mortality have turned me into the man you see now. There is a despair that I must fight, and my impending death which I must triumph over by living fully and achieving until the end. Does this make sense to you?"

"Indeed. I believe that it does." He bowed slightly. "Mr. Flint, I will leave you to your work."

Spock left the lab and turned toward engineering as the doors slid together behind him. He delivered the request for an inventory of substances to Mr. Scott, all the while brooding over his exchange with Flint. Then he headed for the turbolift and his cabin.

The warmth and silence of his quarters were soothing. He sank into his chair and gave himself over to reflection. It was fortunate that Flint had decided to attribute Kirk's lack of hostility to the captain's noble character. It seemed that Flint would force no confrontation or embarrassing discussions with the captain. *Still, it is a time bomb. Even if Flint never brings it up, it's unfair to Jim to keep him in the dark about what happened.*

Spock considered the changes he had observed in Flint, and his mind wandered back to Boaco Six. For Flint, now grave, noble, sad, reminded Spock sharply of old Mayori, the veteran of that planet's long struggle, the oldest member of the Council of Youngers.

Flint had murmured something to himself, as Spock had stood attending him, observing his experiments. A phrase Spock now identified as a Longfellow quote from "The Building of the Ship": "And in the wreck of noble lives/Something immortal still survives."

The mein of both aged men seemed to embody for Spock a tenet of the philosophy of his own world that had been handed down from Surak: the belief that inner peace could be maintained in the face of all external forces. That a person who married his actions to his beliefs, and kept his conscience clear could, in the face of all trials, maintain his center, his balance, his contentment with the change and flux of I.D.I.C. —the Vulcan credo of Infinite Diversity in Infinite Combination.

But for one without this inner certainty, he thought ruefully, who doubts the merit of his actions, no matter what his situation, there could be no rest, no center, no peace.

The Vulcan stroked his chin and wondered what would happen if war broke out between Boaco Six and Boaco Eight, with the great powers of the galaxy arming both sides in the struggle. Surely carnage and escalation would follow, and the destruction of the fragile order of the Boaco Six revolution, Mayori's young program of prison reform along with it.

Spock picked up his Vulcan harp, let his fingers trail once across its strings, and then laid it down again. Mayori's efforts were worth saving. Perhaps it would take the slow, deliberate efforts of Flint to salvage the slow, deliberate efforts of that other veteran of the years.

Yes, Flint's efforts. And those of a captain who was carrying more burdens than he knew or understood. A captain who had to work with Flint, accommodate him. A captain who trusted his first officer implicitly in all things, and yet had been deceived . . . Spock leaned back in troubled thought.

There could be no center, no inner peace for Spock until Jim knew. The captain was agitated, confused; Spock must bear a large measure of the blame. His mind ran back over other times they had discussed sensitive matters, let down their guard enough to expose their frailties and lend each other support. In this very cabin . . . problems had been discussed. What the stiff and clumsy instruments of language could not express was understood between them. What was not understood was felt. He would make a clean confession to his captain.

Chapter Nineteen

IN THE DREAM, Kirk was being gripped by the shoulders and pushed into a chair. The room was blindingly white, and there was a pulsing, swirling light snaking around above him. He stared up at it and could not look away. It drank in his gaze, his thoughts, his feelings. Lab technicians in white coats shoved him down into the chair, over and over. Another technician, who was somehow Flint, stood in a glass booth, watching. Smiling, he turned a large dial. The light over Kirk shone brighter, swirled faster. A humming noise filled his ears and he let loose a violent scream . . .

The room and the chair disappeared, and Kirk was standing in a clearing. Dust blew in the air around him and settled in his hair, on his uniform. Kirk felt tremendously old. The gravity force seemed overwhelming. His back bent under the heavy load of his arms and hands. He felt as if the planet would draw him down, as if his bones and skin and teeth would crumble away into dust.

His focus shifted, and he became aware that he was encircled by angry children. They crawled out of the thick purple underbrush surrounding the clearing, children of all ages, from different planets, looking haggard and dirty. They were armed with stones, and sharpened sticks, and double-pronged knives, and primitive guns. Their eyes were furious.

A girl rose up out of the tall grass to lead them. She wore fatigues and carried a primitive shotgun. She seemed to be Miri . . . and yet was not Miri. Her hair was light blond and lifted high on her head in a ponytail, so that it came cascading down her neck and back. Her eyes were large, her face . . . seemed somehow familiar, and yet Kirk could not focus on it, could not grasp hold of her name. She raised her arm into the air and gave a cry for the children to advance. They crept along the ground, some slithering on their bellies, some on their hands and knees, their weapons in their hands and mouths. They hummed a taunting, menacing children's song to themselves as they moved in, tightening the circle around Kirk. The girl marched, her head in the air, and by her side a mechanical servant hovered, whirring menacingly.

The girl was now dressed in a shimmering gown, her eyes no less angry. "No one orders me!" She raised her fist and gave a cry for the children to fire, to attack . . .

Kirk woke up suddenly, feeling cold and sick.

He felt better once he had showered and dressed. He made his way along the corridor to his first officer's quarters, smiling wanly at passing crewmen. He pushed the buzzer outside Spock's door and pressed his fingers against the bulkhead. As the Vulcan said "Come in," the doors flew open. Spock sat facing

Kirk, almost as if he had been expecting him. Kirk entered. He felt a blast of hot air hit him; the temperature controls in the cabin were set to approximate the desert air of the planet Vulcan.

"Well, Mr. Spock. I see you're off duty."

"Yes, Captain. Until 1400 hours."

"Any progress in Flint's experiments?"

"I should describe the outlook as hopeful, sir." Spock rose to his feet, watching Kirk intently.

"Well, that's good to hear. And I've just checked in with the bridge. Sulu tells me that the *Sparrow* has made several brief recent appearances. We can't pinpoint it, but we're at close range." Kirk paced about the room as he spoke. Then, he finally turned to face his friend.

"Spock. When we last visited Flint's planet . . . something went wrong . . . something happened down there that's veiled for me, that I'm suppressing, somehow. I feel tension with Flint, and some flicker of . . . resentment. I know he was reluctant to give us the ryetalin we needed when we first arrived. But it's more than that that's making me hate him. Yes, I *hate* him! I know there's something more."

Spock nodded slowly. "Yes, Jim. You had an experience on that planet which caused you a considerable amount of pain and stress, in which you felt that Flint manipulated you. You saw him as an opponent. Circumstances . . . have caused this experience to cease to be a memory for you." Then, in a slightly different voice: "You must trust me that it is the best way."

Kirk swallowed. He and Spock were both standing stiffly, not looking at each other directly. At last, Kirk spoke. "The memory has been . . . removed from my mind, then?" The thought could not but disturb him.

"No, Jim. It has been repressed, not erased. It is still in your mind, but blocked by an artificial . . . defense mechanism, so to speak. You were considerably distraught after our first visit to Flint's world, and I . . . chose a course of action that I only fully understand the implications of now." Spock looked down, as if studying the even carpeting beneath his boots.

Silence fell in the warm chamber. To know that one's mind has been entered and tampered with, that bits of memory are beyond reach, is a frightening thing. There was only one soul in the universe who Kirk trusted enough, from whom he could accept such news without anger or protest. He spoke at last.

"All right, Spock," he said mildly. Yet if the memory could not be restored, he at least wanted to know a little more. "But I read the report on the emergency trip to Flint's world. There was a girl, an android. I feel it was somehow involved . . ."

"It was."

"But how? It wasn't human. Yet I feel that there was some relationship involved, she was so . . ." Kirk frowned, shook his head sharply. "How could a cold computer's brain cause emotional tension, emotional involvement? How could it *feel?*"

"Feelings and emotional attachments can sometimes come from unexpected sources, Captain," Spock remarked tonelessly. In his steely gaze, Kirk could decipher nothing. He decided to give up.

"Well, at any rate," he said at last, "this simplifies my relations with Flint. I suppose. At least I have some clue now as to why I keep wanting to rearrange his distinguished face for him. If there are any new breakthroughs in penetrating his cloaking device, I'll be on the bridge." He turned to go. "Oh, and, Spock?"

"Yes, Captain."

"Thanks."

Spock looked down once more. "Perhaps you ought to reprimand me for taking the liberty of—"

"No. Try it again and I'll clobber you. But whatever memory you removed this time . . . it feels right. I'm better off not knowing." Kirk left the cabin.

Spock sank back into his chair. Though he was once again alone, his face still did not betray his great sense of relief that so much worry and uncertainty had been lifted from both their minds. But he picked up the Vulcan harp once again, and this time let its rippling stream of notes fill his cabin.

Violence had been breaking out in bursts on Boaco Six. In skirmishes between council forces and hostile street gangs on the streets of the city of Boa. In a failed attack on the ocean-crossing air-ferry to the other landmass. In a brutal attack on a small farming village.

Who was supplying the weapons for these attacks? How coordinated, how united were they? How much support from the Federation and Boaco Eight did they have? Each burst of shooting or explosion in the city played havoc with Tamara's nerves, as she waited for news of unfolding galactic events. A handful of years ago, they had declared victory, the war won at last! Why did it now seem never ending?

She traveled with old Mayori to the flattened desert plane where the Romulan equipment had been beamed down. The crates were arrayed below them in the blowing dust, as their air-skimmer touched down with a lurch. Agent Tarn had not stayed to say farewell after the shipment's arrival. This did not bode well.

But Mayori was defending the Romulans. "You, who always doubt, Tamara! You thought they would renege on their agreement. But here is the shipment they promised, as large as they promised, and on time."

Tamara helped him down. "The price in argea was high. But if the equipment is all here, it can make the difference. Both in skirmishes here on our world, and against Boaco Eight."

Young guards were standing by the large gray plastic crates as they arrived. They awaited their approach, and then, on a signal from Tamara, they began to pry the crates open with crowbars.

Mayori spoke as they watched. "We need these weapons. But they will not be enough to protect us in a galactic struggle. If the forces of the Federation are brought to bear on us, we need more than arms. We need an ally."

"Iogan is of your mind," Tamara said dully. "Perhaps even now he is negotiating such a deal."

The front of the first large crate finally gave, with an enormous *crack!* Despite her strained and pensive mood, Tamara looked forward to seeing the first gleam of metal within, to seeing the hi-tech Romulan machines wheeled out into the sun.

There was a layer of sawdust within the crate. The guards moved to brush this away, and it came crumbling to the ground.

More sawdust followed, spilling onto the maroon soil about their feet. It rained onto the guards, a quarter of the crate's contents. A shower of rust poured down after it.

Tamara Angel shut her eyes.

On the bridge of the *Enterprise,* Chekov scanned his console and seemed encouraged by what he saw. "The *Sparrow* has appeared three times in the last hour, sir, each appearance not far from the last one. It must be limping along at sub-light speed."

"Good. As it is, we're getting too close to Klingon space again. Let's hope the kids have sense enough not to tempt fate again *that* way. But the *Sparrow*'s failing power doesn't seem to have caused the Flint device to malfunction permanently, does it?"

"No, sir."

Kirk hit the arm of his chair. Damn Komack. They never knew how these things worked at Starfleet Command. "The cloaking device will probably be the last thing to go," he said aloud. "Let's hope their life-support system hasn't gone critical yet. Mr. Sulu, please estimate how much power the *Sparrow* has left to sustain it."

Sulu did some computations for a vessel of the *Sparrow*'s class, and the energy drain the Flint device would put on it. "Well, sir, the kids seem to be running a pretty fuel-efficient ship. But we don't know how much damage the Klingons did to them. Of course, now that they're traveling at sub-light speed, their fuel consumption rate has gone down . . . whatever kind of shape they're in, I'd say they can't have fuel to last more than another twenty-four hours."

"And possibly considerably less than that, correct, Helmsman?"

"Yes, sir."

A pretty yeoman brought Kirk coffee on a tray. He thanked her and sipped at it. "Lieutenant Uhura. Any report from Starfleet Command on the Boacan situation?"

"No, Captain. At least, no new direct reports on the conflict between the two planets. But the Federation has just declared that solar system a major crisis center, instead of a minor one. I've been picking up Starfleet news bulletins which say that the Federation concedes that it has underestimated the importance of the Boacan system. They're going to devote more energy to it, appoint a more important ambassador to Boaco Eight . . . there's going to be a general shake-down. Maybe some policy changes."

Kirk downed the rest of his hot coffee in one convulsive swallow. "Very interesting, Lieutenant. But our changes may come too late. Well, steady as she goes, helm. When Mr. Flint finds a way to penetrate his device, I want us to be bumper to bumper with the *Sparrow*."

Chekov looked around, perplexed. "Sir?"

Kirk smiled. "That's an old English expression. What I mean is, try to guess her heading and stay close to her tail. And let's try not to overshoot. I take it that the *Enterprise* is also traveling at sub–light speed?"

"Yes, sir. We're just feeling our way along."

"Fine." Kirk felt reassured by his talk with Spock. Back in control. Though it was unpleasant to realize that the flashes of nasty memory he'd been having were real, were only part of a disastrous episode in his life. If someone *had* to be the guardian of his most sordid or distressing secrets, too distracting or volatile for him, himself, to know them, he was glad that that someone was Spock. But still, if he could only . . . that girl, or robot or whatever it was . . .

The intercom whistled.

"Captain? Spock here. Mr. Flint has just informed me he has found a substance capable of outlining the *Sparrow* for us. Small fluorescent particles can be easily manufactured aboard the *Enterprise* in large quantities. If we flush them out of the ship, directing them at the *Sparrow*—"

"How do you propose to do that, Mr. Spock?"

"Mr. Scott and Mr. Flint are conferring on what the best method would be. They also have to rig up machinery to manufacture the particles. And they have to prepare the main hangar deck for possible transporter use."

"You want to use the hangar deck as a transporter? That's pretty risky, Spock. We've never done it before, that's not what it was designed for. I know it's possible in theory . . ."

"Mr. Scott seems to feel he can do it, Captain. He's lining the room with magnetic panels, and bringing in equipment kept in storage by the main transporter. We may need to transport the *Sparrow* aboard, as a last resort."

Kirk frowned. "There's no way we can penetrate the Flint device to get inside the *Sparrow* and get life readings on the children, so that we can beam them up individually?"

"No, sir. Getting an outline reading, a tracing of the exterior of the craft, seems the most we can obtain, as long as the children keep the cloaking device on. Unless they leave it off for a significant period of time or communicate with us directly, we cannot lock onto their individual coordinates."

"And you don't think a tractor beam would do it? We couldn't just open the hangar doors and pull the *Sparrow* aboard?"

"It is difficult to say, Captain, whether even a gentle tractor beam wouldn't destroy the *Sparrow*. It is a fragile, lightweight craft, and the odds are high that its structure was weakened in the clash with the Klingons that deprived it of warp drive."

"Better not risk it, then. Our best bet is still to try to get them to turn off the device."

"Indeed. And perhaps they *will* do this, once we've coated their ship with fluorescence and they see that escape is impossible."

"But just in case, you're turning the main hangar deck into an enormous transporter room for the whole *Sparrow*. An ingenious maneuver, Mr. Spock."

"Thank you, Captain. I shall be joining you on the bridge as soon as my services down here are no longer required. Spock out."

Kirk switched off the intercom. It was a relief to know that Spock was supervising the progress. The secret of being a good captain lay largely in being lucky, Kirk modestly reflected. And in having a first mate that one could depend on.

Chapter Twenty

IT WAS A BAD FOOLIE on board the *Sparrow*. Pal had stopped talking long ago. He had spent days whimpering, and whispering to himself, his lips moving but no sound coming out, then had sat for hours immobile, expressionless, catatonic, while events unfolded. Jahn had ripped apart the closet where Pal liked to hide in the main cabin. The boy did not seem to wish to leave it for the other rooms aboard the small ship; he sat huddled in a corner, near Jahn and Rhea, floating in and out of awareness of those around him.

He had been a silent spectator to the commotion when they entered Klingon space; the *Sparrow* had destroyed a robot satellite and a small slave galley ship, while Rhea argued, screamed, pleaded, and was slammed across the room by Jahn, and then had cried and screamed at Pal, grabbing him by his thin shoulders and shaking him. She shook him and shook him and hugged him to her, keening, and Pal had stared off over her shoulder, emotionless, his eyes wide.

Pal had been the silent witness to the croonings, the

whisperings, and the bickerings of Jahn and Rhea, when they argued about direction, and the use of the cloaking device. When they had kissed, pressed against each other, and Rhea pushed Jahn away and threw things at him as he moved toward her, hissing, "Bitch, tease . . . it's no foolie, Rhea. It's not a game anymore." And Rhea had screamed and screamed.

After that, Jahn and Rhea both seemed frightened of each other, and Rhea became subdued, like Pal, and avoided arguing with Jahn. She would sit by herself, brooding, in the *Sparrow*'s other cabin, rarely leaving it to eat, or coax Pal to take some food. She did not protest when Jahn switched off the Flint device, letting the ship drift, fully visible, while he gloated over the amount of energy he was saving with no camouflage and no movement.

When the Klingon ship closed in and opened fire, Rhea came somewhat alive again; she dove for the console, restored invisibility, and plotted a course back the way they had come. There was something strange about the Grups who attacked them; their chatter over the radio was incomprehensible and harsh sounding, their ships of an odd and scary-looking design. The Grups she had known must be mad at them, but surely Jahn was wrong—they would not attack them. They were different from these Grups. She no longer wished to run away, she needed to talk to someone . . .

Jahn let her assess the damage done to the ship without interference. It took a while for the warp drive to go critical—they made it back to Federation space. There was nothing left to eat, and the food computer was shot, but Rhea no longer felt hungry. In quiet tones she conferred with Jahn about what repairs could be made, how long life support would last, stepping over Pal's limp form as he lay on the floor, gazing at the ceiling.

Jahn was lucid for hours at a time, then would suddenly fly off in a rage. A tantrum gripped him as sensors told him that the *Enterprise* was traveling near the *Sparrow,* groping through space for it, probing for it. He realized that there could not be another warp speed getaway.

Rhea's throat felt sandy and parched; the Klingon attack, in addition to poisoning the food system, had left all beverages undrinkable, even water. The life-support system was also damaged, the air was growing thin. Jahn would tease the starship by letting the *Sparrow* appear for moments at a time, as if taunting Grups from within the ruins of the Home World, once again. A snatch of sound, a glimpse, to remind the Grups of his quickness and power. Rhea felt herself hoping he would miscalculate, that the Grups would catch up with them . . . but then Jahn would reactivate the device, and its barrage of illusions would come back into play.

Several hours after conferring with his captain via the intercom, Spock stepped out of the turbolift onto the bridge and reported success.

"Preparations are completed, Captain. We have had to divert a great deal of energy from other systems of the ship to meet our needs. But Mr. Scott has prepared the main hangar deck for the *Sparrow* to be transported aboard. And Mr. Flint and I have rigged the phaser banks so that they will expel fluorescent particles, in concentrated blasts, instead of phaser energy. If we hit the *Sparrow* with one of these blasts, the outline of the ship will be clear."

"Any chance that the fluorescence will hurt the children?"

"None at all, sir."

"Excellent, Mr. Spock." Kirk flipped the intercom switch on the arm of his chair. "Dr. McCoy, have a medical team report to the main hangar deck to see to the immediate needs of the children." He sat back in his chair. "And now," he said softly, "we'll just have to wait for the *Sparrow* to put in another appearance."

They did not have to wait long. After twelve tense minutes, Lieutenant Uhura leapt up and ripped the transmitter from her ear. "Captain! Loud crackling static . . . and yelling coming through one of my channels," she said.

"Let's hear it, Lieutenant."

"Yes, sir." She moved to her panel, her fingers flying. Radio static filled the bridge. Then yelling.

"You'll die, die, die, die, and Pal will die, I'll kill him, my orders . . ." Gasping, choking, punctuated the manic threats . . . "You can follow my orders or get out, ach, off of the ship." The voice became shrill. "And *you* out there, Grups, can you hear me? You trail me, you bastards, you're out to get me . . . but you can't see me, nyah, nyah, nyah, nyah, we'll die first, I'll kill them . . ."

Kirk jumped up. "Lieutenant! Is there any way we can communicate with them?"

Uhura shook her head, her long brown fingers gliding over her computer panel. "No, Captain. I can't even determine the point of transmission. It seems to be coming from two places at once."

"A mirage, caused by the Flint device," Spock said.

"Well, open a channel, Uhura, and aim it at both points of transmission. Send out a wide signal, one that would be easy for anyone in the area to pick up!"

Kirk shouted over the crackling and the crazy threats. Listening carefully, he thought he could also hear someone crying.

"Channel open, sir."

"Listen to me," Kirk yelled. "You're in trouble. We're here to help you. If you can hear me, turn off the cloaking device, and let us transport you on board." But the only reply was silence and the hum of static. Kirk whispered softly, "Did they hear us?"

Rhea felt as though she were trapped inside a nightmare, inside some strange game. She had been pleading with Jahn for hours, softly, meekly, begging him to turn off the Flint device. "It doesn't matter now what they do with us, Jahn. It doesn't matter how much trouble we're in. We're just making it worse, the ship is losing power . . ."

"No!" Jahn screeched, to every plea and protest. "No, no, no, I'll die first. We'll all die. Before I'll let, the bastard, before the bright light, I'll make them, I'll crush, crush their skulls open, before, back on the planet, I'm sorry, I won't let them get me . . . I'm sorry, Miri . . . I didn't mean to hurt you . . . we'll die, die . . ."

She told him to think of Pal. He called her a traitor, asked her if she wanted to go back to the center. To which she had no answer. But she could not stay in this small room, with Pal's blank stare, and Jahn's screams and accusations. She would go mad.

When the calm, even Grup voice filled the cabin, Jahn froze. Rhea turned around sharply to listen to it. It was soothing, somehow familiar, an old Grup promise of rescue and guidance.

"The blond Grup," Rhea whispered through tears. "Miri's friend, the captain."

"He turned us in the first time," Jahn snarled. "He tricked Miri. Mr. Lovey Dovey."

"Turn off the cloaking device," the voice urged, powerfully, hypnotically, and Rhea moved slowly toward the console, where Jahn stood, white and trembling, beads of sweat on his face.

Rhea lunged around him suddenly. Her fingers closed on circuits, she glided a lever down toward her . . . and the device was off.

Just as cleanly and suddenly, Jahn's hand cut through the air and knocked her across the room. "Traitor," he cried, and turned to the console, to restore invisibility.

Rhea came thudding down against the wall where Pal sat quietly, still-rock, gazing at the wall's dull, cold metal, rubbing his hands back and forth across it, his mouth hanging open. Rhea reached up and brushed a lock of hair out of Pal's wide, empty eyes. She stared past him at Jahn, and wondered if she'd done enough, long enough to make a difference.

It shot onto the viewscreen of the bridge like a flash of quicksilver . . . the image of a small Federation ship.

"The *Sparrow!*" Chekov exclaimed. "Less than seventy kilometers away."

As suddenly as it had come, the image of the *Sparrow* winked out. It was replaced with the usual readings of stars in the vicinity. Then, asteroid rubble appeared, spread across the area which the ship had occupied.

"This, too, is a mirage," Spock said firmly.

"Ignore it," Kirk ordered. "Plot the probable immediate heading of the *Sparrow.*"

"Plotted, sir," Sulu yelled.

"Fire main phaser banks," Kirk commanded.

Sulu seemed to hesitate a fraction of a second, as if afraid that the phaser banks would fire as they normally did and rip the small craft apart. Then he complied. A concentrated stream of swirling pink and blue light shot out of the *Enterprise,* splashing and dispersing in the void of space. The light passed through the illusion of asteroid debris and continued disbanding into space. Suddenly, amid the asteroid rubble, a superimposed glowing image of the prow of a ship became apparent.

"We winged it!" Kirk said, pleased. "We got a piece of it."

Spock bent over his computer viewer at his science panel. "It will take a few moments for our banks of fluorescent particles to recharge."

"Captain," Chekov said, "there is a large Klingon wessel not far away, just inside the parameter of Klingon space."

"Waiting to come after the spoils, if we give up or fail," Kirk said grimly. "But we got here first. They're not getting these children."

The doors of the turbolift flew open and Flint entered the bridge. "Captain Kirk, I would be grateful for the chance to watch the final execution of the experiment from the bridge, if you will permit it."

Kirk gazed at him steadily. "Sir, we are honored to have you here."

Flint inclined his head. "I thank you. The fluorescent particles should by now be ready to be discharged for a second time."

"Confirmed," Spock said from his panel.

"Fire main phasers, then," Kirk ordered.

Another burst of pastel light issued forth from the starship, and seemed to gather and take shape in the vacuum of space. Now, through the translucent false image of the asteroids, the complete outline of a ship could be seen, shimmering and pulsing with light.

"Got it, sir! A direct hit," Chekov yelled, but his brow quickly clouded with consternation. "Captain. The Klingon ship is *leaving* Klingon space and moving toward us at warp five."

Kirk drank this news in, stunned. It spelled crisis, reckless aggression, an ultimatum . . . he switched the intercom so he had a direct tie-in with the main hangar deck. "Mr. Scott," he said tensely, "prepare to beam the *Sparrow* aboard."

"Captain," Scotty cried out, "I canna do it so quickly. To transport a ship of this size on board, I'll have to divert more power from other sources. I've got men working on it now. We couldn't do it earlier, when you needed power to fire the phasers."

"Hurry, Scotty," Kirk urged.

"Klingon ship approaching, decreasing its speed," Sulu reported.

Kirk beckoned his first officer toward him. "Spock. Do you think the Klingons could want an all-out confrontation? Galactic war?"

"Possibly, Captain. Their intent could be to provoke us and create an inflammatory incident. Or they *may* see what we're up to. They *may* only want the *Sparrow*."

"And if we let them have it," Kirk said slowly, "we might avert catastrophe."

"We must proceed with caution," Spock said, "at such a sensitive time. Rumors of a Klingon-Romulan alliance might have some truth to them. The Federation must not stumble into conflict against such a formidable coalition."

"I quite agree," Kirk said.

A storm of sputtering came from the area near the door of the turbolift. Once again, Ensign Michaels was breaking with protocol and regulations, and making his presence known. "You're going to let the Klingons take them? Let the Klingons saunter into our space and claim these mixed-up kids? You can't be serious, sir."

"Quiet, Ensign," Kirk said. "We're not giving away anything unless we have to." Under his breath he urged, "C'mon, Scotty. C'mon."

The intercom whistled. Scott's familiar brogue sounded confident. "We're ready now, Captain. Standing by to beam the *Sparrow* aboard . . ."

An ugly white beam shot out of the Klingon ship. It blasted into the graceful metal arch that lifted up the cylindrical top decks of the *Enterprise*. The bridge shook. It was a well-aimed shot. The neck of the ship was a technical nerve center; Kirk prayed that the damage was not severe. Reports of injuries began to flood Uhura's channels.

"Shields up!" Kirk barked hoarsely. "Drop everything, Mr. Scott. Divert all power back if you have to, but *get those shields up!*"

"Aye, sir."

"The answer to our question, Captain," Spock said, as he helped a shaken Flint rise to his feet. "They feel confident enough to risk an all-out war."

"Mr. Sulu," Kirk said quietly, "sound the red alert."

The insistent siren's wail pierced every deck, corridor, and corner of the *Enterprise*. And with it came her captain's voice. "Red alert. Red alert. All hands to battle stations. This is not a drill. I repeat. This is *not* a drill."

Chapter Twenty-one

THE WAITING WAS MADDENING.

"Analysis, Mr. Spock?"

"I believe the shot was intended to divert us from rescuing the *Sparrow,* not to engage us in battle. They may not fire another shot."

"But if they do, we're helpless. Can we fire phasers against them?"

Spock and Flint exchanged glances. Then Spock shook his head. "No, sir. The phaser apparatus is still rigged to fire fluorescent particles. The possible imminence of a battle did not occur to us when we were adapting it."

"There was no reason why it should have. So all we've got, right now, are photon torpedoes?"

"Yes, Captain. But as the torpedoes are energy efficient, in terms of launching them, we could probably safely fire one before Mr. Scott finishes his readjustments."

Kirk confirmed this with Scotty. "Mr. Sulu, fire one photon torpedo past the right side of the Klingon ship, as a warning shot. Make sure you do not injure the Klingon ship."

Once more, Michaels burst the quiet tension of the room. "One torpedo? Wasted on purpose? They attacked us. They're testing your resolve. And you're playing games with them?"

"Ensign Michaels, you are relieved of duty. Report to your quarters and stay there." Without waiting to watch the young man register this and comply, Kirk repeated, "Fire, Mr. Sulu."

As the turbolift doors whooshed shut on Michaels, a tight ball of flame shot out of the wounded arching neck of the *Enterprise* and sailed past the right wing of the Klingon vessel.

"Now," Kirk said, "let's hope they don't call our bluff."

The viewscreen of the *Sparrow* had afforded the tiny ship a panoramic view of the fluorescence shooting toward it. Soon the ship was enveloped, and the screen showed the stars and the *Enterprise* through a veil of pink and purple. Jahn swore, exclaimed that he'd been tagged, been marked. Rhea simply closed her eyes in gratitude that her move had been enough, that they were invisible no longer.

The fluorescence soaked through the hull of the ship, giving the room a curious ghostly glow. It was a comforting light; they had been in the eye of a storm, and now, it seemed to Rhea, they were in the eye of a rainbow, a nexus of color.

Through the shimmering haze, Jahn cheered on a battle in space that appeared on the screen, but at the sight of the Klingon ship, Rhea's heart sank. It was the same scary-looking kind of ship as had attacked them when they wandered into the other space. It had come after them. Even if the blond Grup was their friend, even if he was ready to forgive them, something told her that these other Grups would not.

"The Klingons have put up their shields," Sulu reported.

"Uhura, open a channel to the Klingon ship. Let's make them think we feel strong enough to bargain."

"Aye, aye, Captain. Stand by for audio-visual contact."

Once more the smirking face of Commander Kreth appeared on the main screen.

"Well, Kirk. You do not seem to have activated your shields. You enjoy living dangerously?"

"You must enjoy living dangerously, Kreth. What are you doing in Federation star space? And our shields are down because we've got some transporting to do."

"Do you indeed. It was very obliging of you to outline the form of the renegade Federation ship, which entered Klingon space for its attacks, so that we may now claim it and the saboteurs on board. And we want to investigate this interesting way you seem to have thwarted your own new cloaking device."

"Cossack," Chekov muttered, under his breath.

Kreth crept across his bridge with the easy assurance of a tarantula in its lair. In a chair by the wall sat Iogan, the young boy minister from Boaco Six. His eyes followed Kreth's form, then flicked to a young Klingon who sat near him. On the young Klingon's face the skin in places appeared raised in bubbles. Kirk knew this meant that the crewman had been punished for some breach of regulations with an atom-air gun, a horribly painful Klingon device for maintaining discipline. It shot gas into the skin of the victim, causing cells to rupture, explode. Kirk hoped the young Boacan had been on hand when the punishment was administered. It would give him some insight into his Klingon "friends."

Kirk stared calmly at Kreth. "The Federation will take responsibility for this small ship. Your claims for justice will be heard in due course by the Council of the Federation of Planets," he said firmly.

Kreth snorted. "We prefer to procure justice for ourselves." He narrowed his eyes at Kirk. "Why did you fire a torpedo at us, just now, instead of using phasers?"

"To show you we mean business. That we're willing to fight if you are." Silently Kirk prayed that Kreth would not take him up on this. Without shields, without phasers, the *Enterprise* did not stand a chance. In his mind, Kirk pictured his majestic silver ship being ripped apart by Klingon phasers. He would be almost powerless to respond.

Finally, Kreth responded. "There is no need for us to fight, Captain. Why, we have no quarrel with you. Only with the pirates in that small ship. Do not interfere, and there will be no trouble. Kreth out." His image winked off the screen.

The crew on board the bridge of the *Enterprise* gave a collective sigh of relief. Kirk's bluff had apparently worked.

"A well-played hand, Captain," said Flint.

"Mr. Scott," Kirk yelled into the intercom, "we need those shields, and that phaser power!"

"We're going as fast as we can, Captain. But that one Klingon phaser blast was well placed. It sliced into one of our generator units. I'm going to have to redivert power around it. I'm switching life support, and other of the ship's functions, onto impulse power. But it'll take some time."

"Time is what we don't have, Scotty. Kirk out."

"Captain, look!" Chekov said, and Kirk looked up. A new horror was being acted out in space. A tractor beam reached out of the Klingon ship and clutched the *Sparrow,* drawing it inexorably toward the Klingon bird of prey.

"A tractor beam? They're crazy!" Kirk cried.

"A high-intensity tractor beam, Captain," Spock confirmed. "The *Sparrow* cannot possibly stand the strain."

"Lieutenant Uhura! Put me through to the Klingon ship again." Kirk rose. "Kreth, you bloody fool. You'll destroy the ship, *and* the cloaking device you want so badly. You'll kill the children. You'll accomplish nothing."

"The Klingons will not respond or acknowledge, Captain," Uhura said.

"Then tie me in with the *Sparrow* again." Kirk tightened and untightened his fists in frustration.

"They don't acknowledge, either."

"Doesn't matter. Doesn't matter. Keep the channel open, Lieutenant." Kirk was sweating. He swallowed hard. *What are the children's names? A good, calm, authoritative voice.* "Pal. Jahn. Rhea. Listen to me. Your ship is about to be destroyed by a Klingon tractor beam. We offer you food and protection, clean air, comfort, safety, guidance. Please turn off your cloaking device, so that we can beam you aboard."

A Klingon phaser blast shot out and grazed the cylindrical smooth top decks of the *Enterprise,* not far from the bridge.

Flint shook his head as the crew steadied itself from

the shock. "They're warning you, Captain. They must be intercepting your message."

"Turn off the cloaking device, children," Kirk repeated evenly. "I'm here to help you. You have nothing to fear. We want to put things right, to protect you."

Within the alien tractor beam, the small ship seemed to twist and buckle and writhe like a small animal in a trap. How long before it gave?

Mr. Scott called up to the bridge. "Captain, we have shield capacity again. And phaser power, though there may be some of that fluorescent rubbish mixed in with it. Shall I put up the shields?"

"Negative, Scotty. Can you transport?"

"Aye, a few individual people from the *Sparrow,* I can, but not the whole beastie, not anymore."

"Very good, Mr. Scott. Stand by in the transporter room to bring the children on board, if they turn off their cloaking device. We've got to be quick—the Klingons may try to beam them aboard first. So we've got to make sure that our beam is the one to lock onto them."

"Aye, Captain. Standing by."

Spock approached Kirk's command chair. "The Flint device may fail on its own, from the strain of the tractor beam. But even if it does, or if the children turn it off . . ."

"Yes, Mr. Spock?"

"Transporting children out of a high-intensity Klingon tractor beam . . . they might not pull through."

"The risk is noted," Kirk said. "But there seems little choice. This is their one chance of survival. They'll die in the tractor beam. They'll die if the Klingons get them. If they turn off the cloaking device,

212

we'll try to beam them aboard. It's up to the Onlies now."

Kirk had Uhura tie him in once more to the *Sparrow,* and recommenced urging them with a steady stream of pleading and reason.

When the Klingon tractor beam reached the *Sparrow,* there was a jolt, and then the little ship seemed to come alive. Every panel, every pastel glowing wall, every fiber and circuit began to groan and whine and tremble, to shift uneasily. The cabin began to heat up.

"They've got us!" Jahn screamed. "Someone's got us, leggo, leggo, we're trapped, they know where we are."

The lights in the cabin flickered, warning alarms sounded, the machinery snapped and popped and short-circuited.

As Kirk's voice filled the cabin once again, Jahn began to laugh. He laughed and swore, and the walls began to creak and give; the hull of the *Sparrow* was cracking and folding in on itself. The main panel exploded in a fireworks display. There was a burst of smoke, a hiss, a sickening smell. And after the smoke cleared, there was Jahn, lying on the floor, his head askew, his face half scorched, his eyes rolled back. Now Jahn lay still-rock, his mouth contorted, as dead as a Grup or an Only gone bad.

Rhea screamed. And then rose. She approached the panel which was still smoldering, spitting energy. She would listen to reason, as the Grup's voice urged, and surrender the ship. But the panel was destroyed, the mechanisms jammed. Communications were inoperable. And the Flint device could not be deactivated. Kirk's pleading could no longer be heard.

"Pal," Rhea said cheerfully, "I'm going to open the

door now." Jahn had sealed them all into the main cabin. Life supports in the sleeping chamber were shut down. But Rhea could tell from a chart by the door that they could make it the short distance down the corridor to the transporter booth. She could feel the cabin floor becoming warmer, hard to walk on, through the soles of her boots. The overhead light had failed, but she could still see by the light of the glowing fluorescent walls. She continued to draw comfort from this light; it warmed her in the same way as had the soft-spoken praise she sometimes got from Mrs. File, back at the Center. She could not go back there now, but she would do what this light, what this warm feeling inside, seemed to be telling her to do.

Rhea dug her fingernails into the space between the cabin's main doors, and pulled. The doors trembled, the mechanism buzzed. At last, with a groan, the doors slid open.

The giant Klingon ship was looming ever larger on the viewscreen, its hangar doors open like a hungry mouth. Rhea ran over to Pal, scooped up his limp form, and slung it over her shoulder. She carried him out the cabin door, down the corridor, to the transporter pad. By pressing against the wall of the corridor, she nimbly avoided a ceiling panel as it crashed down, clattering to the floor, as the ship continued to moan and shift. She lay Pal down on the transporter pad, activated the monitor, and frowned. Barely enough power left to transport one person. Well, it would have to do. More explosions, and the smell of smoke floated from the main cabin. "Hang on, Pal. Hang on."

The hot floor beneath her feet was heaving, buckling. She used sensors to gauge the coordinates of the

Enterprise transporter room. It was primed for beam-up. Well, she'd give it something to lock on to.

It was then that the roof fell in, bringing the icy emptiness of space in its wake. The *Sparrow* shuddered, collapsed inward.

With a loud cry of pain and terror mixed with triumph, Rhea moved the levers of the transporter console down, and Pal's small body dazzled and dissolved. Then the good ship *Sparrow* lost its cloaking capability. The illusion of asteroid rubble melted away. The ship imploded in a brilliant show of fluorescence, fire, and metal shards.

On the bridge of the *Enterprise,* Kirk shut his eyes. "Oh, God," he whispered.

"An admirable attempt, Captain," Flint said. The sound of his voice made Kirk feel sick.

A stiff hand rested awkwardly on Kirk's shoulder for a moment, then withdrew. "The end of many trials, Jim," Spock said softly.

The Vulcan's presence steadied Kirk as it had many times before.

"Yes, Mr. Spock. And the beginning of others, I expect. But at least it seems that the Klingons have overplayed their hand."

The *Enterprise* shifted from a state of red to yellow alert. And down in the transporter room, Mr. Scott was mightily surprised to find a small boy curled up on a transporter pad, staring up at nothing.

Chapter Twenty-two

THE DAMAGE TO THE *Enterprise,* it turned out, had been minimal. There were no fatal injuries. McCoy and his capable team soon had the casualties well in hand. There was no need to stop off at a space station or a starbase; complete repairs could be effected on board within the space of a day.

After the implosion of the *Sparrow,* the Klingon ship had turned off its tractor beam, scanned the shards and debris that floated aimlessly in the void, and then retreated rather sheepishly back into Klingon space. Kirk knew that this would finish Kreth's career. Such mistakes were not easily forgiven by the empire.

A late crisis report came in; the door of an auxiliary control room was jammed, and two crewmen were trapped inside the smoke-filled room. Kirk went down to observe as a security team blasted the doors open, phasers ripping into the high-density metal, slowly eating through. The team dove inside and pulled the choking men out to safety. They were run down to sickbay.

Once repairs were well under way, and Mr. Scott could be spared from engineering, Kirk left him in charge of the bridge. Then he headed down to sickbay himself, to join a serious and perplexed group that had gathered there.

"Bones, how's the boy?"

"Well," McCoy grumbled, "it's been hard to find time to attend to him, we've been so busy patching up the people who got too close to those two Klingon phaser blasts. Do me a favor, Jim. Next time our shields aren't working, don't thumb your nose at the Klingons. We don't need this much excitement down here in sickbay . . ."

"Bones, stop blithering and tell me. The boy, Pal. How is he? Was he seriously injured?"

They had moved into the room where Pal lay. The readings on the life-support monitor above his small body rose and fell as he breathed, and as they indicated different bodily organs and systems. Nurse Chapel, Dr. Ramsey, Spock, and Flint stood by the bed watching the readings.

McCoy sighed. "Well, physically he seems all right. He's inhaled some nasty fumes, but nothing noxious, nothing he won't work right out of his system. He's underfed and dehydrated, hasn't eaten or drunk for a few days. And he's exhausted, of course. But we're compensating for all that. And none of it accounts for his current state."

"Which is?"

"Near catatonia, Jim. I've had Ramsey here, and some of the other child specialists in to look at him, but they don't have a clue, can't get through to him. The boy could, of course, just be in a state of shock. Shell-shocked." McCoy shook his head, and lowered his voice to a near whisper, perhaps so that Dr.

Ramsey could not hear. "I'd sure hate to return this kid to that program on his planet though, in his current condition. Especially with that guy Voltmer in charge. Nothing that I've read about the boy or was told while we were there shows that they had any understanding that he was this disturbed."

"He may not have been, Bones. We can't know what he's been through this last week or so. How the fight in the children's recreation room and being kidnapped affected him. Or what went on aboard the *Sparrow.*"

"Yes, of course. I'm sure he was a much saner child before this all began. But my point is, he needs therapy, he needs sensitive, reliable care. And I'm not convinced that he's gonna get it back on Juram Five. Wish there was something we could do for him, here and now."

Kirk could see that Spock was glancing over at them. Were his Vulcan ears picking up the doctor's whispered remarks?

"No change, Doctor," Nurse Chapel said. "He simply stares off into space . . . shall I give him a rest injection?"

"Yes, Christine. I think that would be best. Sleep may do that child a world of good."

Pal did not move as Nurse Chapel lifted the hypo to his arm, or when it hissed the soothing liquid into his bloodstream. After a few moments, his pallid eyelids closed.

The adults adjourned to the next room, to continue their discussion.

"Tragic, Captain," Ramsey said. "Simply tragic. Heaven knows what went on aboard that ship, what abuse that boy was exposed to. Dr. Voltmer has wired me about how dangerous those two older Onlies were. Degenerate and violent."

"Yes, well. At least one of those violent degenerates was apparently sane and considerate enough to sacrifice self and beam Pal onto the *Enterprise*," Kirk said.

"We may never know the full story unless Pal snaps out of it," McCoy remarked. "Surely it's important that we find out."

"Keep me updated, Bones," Kirk said, heading out the door, anxious to return to the bridge and relieve Mr. Scott. Spock followed him.

Kirk and Spock returned to sickbay the following afternoon, at McCoy's request. The captain visited with the crewmen who had been injured during the Klingon attack, and then headed into the room where Pal lay. Flint was there also, and it irritated Kirk—why was the man always hovering, always underfoot? But the famed recluse had been tasting again, for the first time in many decades, what total immersion in the society of other people felt like.

He had been frequenting all decks, and Spock, by special request, had taken him on a tour of every recreational, cultural, and social facility on board the *Enterprise*. Libraries and workshop classes, gymnasiums and concerts, the chapel and the dance center . . . And Flint had expressed a wish to visit Juram Five, to see the Onlies' Center, see how the children were being raised. So the *Enterprise* was under orders to return Flint to his planet only after Pal had been returned to his.

"Good afternoon, Captain."

Kirk smiled. "Good afternoon, Mr. Flint."

"I trust I am not making a nuisance of myself. The boy's case interests me."

"Not at all, sir. Dr. McCoy, how is your patient at the moment? Any improvement?"

219

"Perhaps you'd better see for yourself, Jim." McCoy led the way back into Pal's room. The boy lay on the bed, still immobile, with his eyes now open, an indication that the rest injection had worn off. He rarely blinked. Kirk knew that McCoy wanted to impress on him how helpless, how pathetic the boy was, how disastrous it would be to return him to the care of incompetents.

Nurse Chapel stood at Pal's bedside and sponged his forehead with a cool compress.

"You see, Jim?" McCoy said. "Same as last night. We're not sure when he woke up, if you could call it that, but he's just been lying there . . . I'd like more time to look into this."

"I'm sorry, Bones, but there isn't much time. We're in no particular hurry, but after we drop off Pal and Mr. Flint I have orders to head back to the Boacan system, to try to iron things out and pick up where we left off. I don't think we can be too leisurely about it. And even traveling at just warp three, we'll reach the Onlies' planet sometime tomorrow."

"Damn," said McCoy. "I just don't feel good about leaving the boy there, and sailing on. I wish we could get some answers. But there's just no way to reach him."

Spock stepped forward and cleared his throat. "There is a way, of course, Doctor. And I am willing to volunteer my services in this effort."

Nurse Chapel dropped her compress, then nervously set it on the bedside tray. Everyone, with the exception of the motionless patient, turned to look at Spock.

"I wasn't hinting at that, Spock," McCoy protested. "Or suggesting it in any way."

"I am sure you were not, Doctor. But it does seem the logical course for us to follow. Even if you had a few more days at your disposal, it is doubtful whether you could learn anything of significance, or break through to the boy."

"Thanks for the vote of confidence," McCoy muttered.

"I merely point out that there is a quicker, more efficient method at our disposal."

Kirk wavered. "We can't ask you to do this, Spock. There are specialists trained to deal with this kind of thing . . ."

"Who could not get through to Pal's mind as directly or as easily as I can. Please, Captain. I considered this at great length last night. I, too, am curious to know more about this problem."

"Very well, Mr. Spock," Kirk said.

Nurse Chapel moved away from the bed to allow Spock access to the child. Spock shut his eyes for a moment of concentration. He flexed the long thin fingers of his hands. With subtle, deft movements, the fingers of his right hand glided along the scalp-line and the ear of the boy. His left hand quivered and secured a hold on Pal's forehead, pressing in at the temples and around his eye socket. Pal showed no awareness of his presence.

Spock's face became strangely hunted, haunted. He brought it down close to the boy's. "Our minds are one . . ." he whispered. He shuddered, the only indication he gave of the struggle now going on inside him. The Vulcan mind-meld demanded that the fiercely private Spock make himself completely vulnerable, lower his psychological barriers layer by layer, even as it demanded that Pal lower his. "Our thoughts . . . becoming one . . ." Spock urged hypnotically, ". . . our minds . . ." His words drifted off into silence.

After a minute or two, he whimpered. His eyes darted around feverishly, defensive, like a small boy's. "Hide, curl up," said the stranger's voice that spoke through his mouth, "ball up like an Only in a ball, hide from the bright light . . . and his arm came off. Dr. Nazafar-7's arm . . . a very bad citizen . . . and then the snakes come down, they come spinning down to get you . . ." Spock's words crumbled into incoherence and he started, twitched several times.

Minutes ticked by. Kirk became concerned. Surely Spock had maintained the mind-meld for too long. Surely it was time for him to snap out of it. There was a danger, Kirk knew, of two minds, two personalities drowning in each other if it went on too long, of the telepath being drawn so deeply into another's thoughts, merging so completely, that he couldn't get back out. Vulcans trained hard when they were young, to be able to maintain discipline and self-control, even during a mind-meld. But Spock was half—human . . .

"Spock," he said finally. "Spock, come out of it."

His friend continued to talk to himself and dart his eyes about, oblivious to Kirk and the others in the room.

"Spock!" Now Kirk ran and pried the skinny hands from the child's head, grabbed Spock by the shoulders and shook him. "Snap out of it. Get hold of yourself!" *Literally,* he thought. The form he held sagged and swayed, its face dangerously pale.

Then the science officer straightened and shook himself, as if shaking off a heavy cloak. His face regained its usual slightly green tinge. He looked around the room. "There is no need for concern, I assure all of you. I am quite myself again. And Pal, I trust, is somewhat healed and more whole than he was before."

They all glanced down at the boy, who lay with his eyes shut tight.

"What was it, Spock, that hurt him? Was it the shock of all the violence?" asked McCoy.

"A combination of disturbing experiences, Doctor. Obviously, many have occurred during the last few weeks, and I believe I could now reconstruct those for you. Some of Pal's maladjustment seems unavoidable. The centuries of living among the Onlies, aging hardly at all, and his recent sudden spurt of growth"—Spock avoided Flint's gaze—"have unbalanced him, and so has the great switch in life-styles."

Spock paused meaningfully. "However. There is much more to it. Pal is a strong and vital child, with a fine intelligence. But his mind has been entered before. More deeply than most telepaths would consider ethical. And it was *not* entered by a trained telepath. It was entered and severely tampered with by a clumsy and insensitive machine."

"The chair in Voltmer's laboratory," Kirk said bitterly.

"Yes, Captain. Used for much more than he wished us to believe. Pal's mind has been probed so deeply that many memories and many vital experiences have been completely erased. The machine has clumsily tried to reconstruct and create some memories in his mind, in order to promote what Voltmer considers 'right' thinking. Fears have been placed in the child's mind to promote discipline. For example, in order to discourage Pal from hoarding food in his closet at the

Center, something he was fond of doing, an image was placed in his mind of a large, coiled, venomous snake poised to strike any who engaged in such activities."

McCoy whistled. "Voodoo psychology. This should finish Voltmer when it gets out. If he isn't finished already."

"I must agree with you, Doctor. Abuses of this kind need to be made public."

"And you've reached Pal now?" Kirk asked. It was hard to tell if the boy's condition had improved. He had tucked his head under his arm and lay still, as if either stupified or frightened.

"Yes, Captain. He is reorienting himself, his persona, after this especially lengthy melding experience. The disturbance in his mind was so great that the boy was losing ground to schizophrenia. The healthy, lively Pal, who had weathered so many centuries, was frightened by the artificial experiences and emotions the machine tried to graft onto his mind. He retreated into an infantile, subdued state. I have reached him, his voice, his center . . . he is by no means perfectly well, but I believe he is on the road to recovery."

Pal was gradually becoming aware of the adults and their talk. This became apparent as he cautiously lifted his head and peered up at them. When all eyes focused on him, expectantly, he sat up and suddenly burst into tears. Nurse Chapel walked to him confidently, scooped up his shuddering body, and pressed his head against her neck. Through his convulsive sobs, they were at last able to make out the word *hungry*. A lab assistant was sent to get some mild broth. Talk stopped for a moment, as the other adults watched the ancient, strange little gnome of a boy, pleased to see him behaving like a child at last.

"Yes, I believe he'll be all right now," McCoy said. "Thanks to you and that Vulcan magic, Spock."

"I assure you, Doctor," Spock said gravely, "that no magic is involved. The principles behind telepathy are entirely scientific. I shall explain them to you, sometime."

"Now, hold on a minute, Spock. Don't get too pleased with yourself. Sometimes I think you're after my job."

The two men continued bickering as Kirk chuckled, and Flint watched Pal as he howled, and Nurse Chapel rocked him, smoothed his hair, and shushed him.

Chapter Twenty-three

Mrs. File was a large, cheerful, comfortable woman with gray hair that hung down her back in a neat braid. She wore old-fashioned eyeglasses and smelled of violet water. She had been left in charge of the Children's Center until a replacement for Voltmer could be found. Ramsey quietly relayed to Kirk a rumor that there was a proposal to make her position permanent. Ramsey's own admiration for Voltmer had waned as the full extent of his abuses became known.

Mrs. File and her staff met Kirk and the men who had come down with him in the recreation room. It seemed greatly changed to Kirk. It was cheerfully lit, and light poured through its large fiberglass windows. A light that was natural. And not too bright. It had been a gray day the last time Kirk visited this place. In every possible way.

But it was the presence of the Onlies in the room that really altered it, made it seem a completely different place. They shouted to each other, and argued and giggled and squealed as they played on the floor, wrestling, building block towers and crystal jigsaw towers, challenging each other to pocket laser-set battles, building bridges between the low tables and the children-size chairs out of stretch string.

A few pressed their faces against the windows, stared out at the land covered with moss and ferns. It was land that had been scarred, devastated during the war of the adults, and that over the centuries nature had reclaimed. The Children's Center was built hundreds of miles from the city in which they had lived as scavengers during those years.

As Kirk looked about him, he remembered the faces, even the names of some of them. And how they had looked when he first encountered them, grimy and smudged and dressed in rags. They had been distrustful of the Grups from the *Enterprise*, and slowly given their trust. How remarkable that they could still trust adults, could still enjoy themselves, lose themselves in play, after the betrayals they'd known here. The stubborn childish determination to live, and love. An ash-blond little girl had thrown her arms around his legs when he arrived, and many of the children greeted him cheerfully, and with recognition.

Spock was standing by Mrs. File with his hands clasped together behind his back, relating to her how Rhea had saved Pal in her final moments. Though Pal had seemed unaware and unresponsive at the time, his memory had recorded it.

"Yes, Rhea was a courageous girl, and very gifted," the woman said. "The sheer stupidity of such a loss, such an utter waste is what baffles me the most."

Kirk, gazing round, became preoccupied once again with another baffling loss. The death of another

227

courageous Only. As if reading his thoughts, a boy of thirteen or so, physically, with a pinched freckled face, walked up to Kirk and said accusingly, "You're Miri's Grup, aren't you? But you never came back to see her. She said you would come for her one day and take her away from here."

"Tomi," Mrs. File said quickly, "go see if you can help those little fellows make a hammock out of stretch string." She bustled him off toward the cluster of smaller boys and turned back to Kirk apologetically.

"You know, Captain Kirk, Miri did often speak of you, but I believe she was happy on the Program, and she was planning next year to go away to school to train to be a teacher. Your influence on her and the other children was only positive."

Kirk knew her words were meant to take the sting out of what the boy had said. She couldn't know how badly it stung. Glancing around the room again, Kirk saw Flint on the floor with some of the youngest children, looking ridiculous and undignified in a floppy green hat, apparently engaged in a game of peekaboo. The sight did not lift Kirk's spirits.

"Yes," he said. "Well. I take it that the chair in the 'treatment room' is being dismantled?"

Mrs. File's face clouded. "Yes, it has been dismantled, Captain. And I must assure you that I and the rest of the staff had no idea of the extent to which Dr. Voltmer was abusing the minds of the children. Though we did suspect, somewhat, I suppose. It explains much of their erratic behavior. Makes things clearer. Voltmer is on Starbase Twelve now, waiting to stand trial for malpractice, falsifying records, perhaps even child abuse."

Kirk pictured Voltmer's fleshy face and ingratiating smile. He imagined the man standing before a Federation subcommittee hearing charges read against him. It brought Kirk a dull satisfaction, to think of it.

Mrs. File turned to Spock. "Your report on the damage done to Pal's mind was most enlightening. It appears, Captain, that once again the Onlies are greatly indebted to you and your men."

Kirk's eyes found Pal sitting in a corner of the room, piling glo-rocks in a bucket with several little girls. "Take care of them," he said softly to Mrs. File. He flipped open his communicator. "Mr. Scott. Stand by to beam up the landing party."

McCoy had found his conversations with the staff of the Children's Center interesting and informative. He felt sure that Pal was now in sensitive, caring hands. The children were being questioned about their experiences in Voltmer's chair, something Voltmer had discouraged when he was in charge. A formal investigation, on the strength of Spock's report, was under way.

The doctor felt eager to discuss some of what Mrs. File had told him with the captain. But when he called up to the bridge from sickbay, Spock was in command. The *Enterprise* was heading back toward Flint's private planet to return their remarkable guest to his study, solitude, and creative work.

Kirk's absence from the bridge made McCoy feel uneasy. Spock had taken the doctor aside and mentioned to him days earlier that Kirk and Spock had been talking; the captain now knew something of what had occurred on Flint's planet, and he accepted not knowing everything. His peace of mind had improved; but he still seemed depressed, moody, during their visit to the planet of the Onlies. McCoy left Nurse Chapel in charge of sickbay once again, and set out in search of Kirk.

The captain was not in his quarters, not in a recreation room or the gym, not in the main library or gardens, or in his favorite mess hall. McCoy found him at last on the ship's largest observation deck. The cavernous room was dark, and the cool air blew through it as if through an empty stadium. The walls were windows, encasing darkness and flecks of light, the galaxy dizzyingly receding around it on all sides. The giant room was simply constructed to be an amphitheater for the stars.

The lone figure it contained looked as small as a gladiator in a giant ring. Kirk was leaning his hand against one of the colossal windows. In his other hand he held a long tall glass of Rigellian whiskey. McCoy walked toward him, and his footsteps, his voice when he spoke, echoed through the chamber.

"Is this a private party, Captain? Or can anyone drink away his troubles here?"

Kirk did not look at him. "Well, Doctor. You've found me out, have you?"

"Looks like it. There were a few things I wanted to discuss with you, pass on to you. But they can wait."

Now Kirk turned to face him. "No, no. Tell me. I'm interested."

McCoy scratched his head. "Well, it's just that I had a talk with Mrs. File, while we were on the planet. About the question of how fast the Onlies age, among other things. She said that in the future it will be up to the children themselves, whether they decide to stay children, or whether they choose to take the shots to make them grow. She says that a surprising number say they want to grow up *now*. Pal included."

After mulling this over, Kirk asked, "And what did she have to say about Pal, about his condition?"

"Why, she says he seems to be in better shape now than he was in before he was kidnapped by the Onlies who stole the *Sparrow*. Apparently, Spock's mind-meld undid a great deal of the damage done by Voltmer and his cronies, with their chair."

"Good, good." Kirk took another drink of whiskey.

McCoy hesitated, then told him the next bit of news. "File also said they're looking into the possibility of homes for some of the Onlies that plan on growing up at a normal rate—sending them to a foster family environment, away from the Center. Since the Center doesn't seem to be doing them all that much good. And Flint—"

Kirk's eyes flicked to meet his.

"Flint has expressed an interest to me in adopting Pal. Helping the boy adjust from seeming immortality to the process of aging. He says that it's a process that he himself knows and understands, now."

"Flint?" Kirk said. "Thinks he can raise a child alone on that cold, dry, sad planet of his?"

"Well, I saw him playing with some of the children, Jim. There may be more fun in him than you realize."

"Yes, I saw him too. Are you sure his sudden rapid aging hasn't made him senile? Does he want Pal to share his second childhood with him? Is that it?" Kirk heard the bitterness and rancor in his voice and it startled him. He looked down. "I'm not being fair, Bones. And I know it."

"You must remember," McCoy said gently, "that all his sons and daughters on Earth have long since died, centuries ago. And Flint has not dared to stay in touch with their descendants. Any of us could be of his family. None of us is, for certain."

"Of course, Bones, of course. I'm hardly an objective judge or a worthy judge of such a great man. And I can barely back up a single negative thing that I might say about him." Kirk laughed hollowly, then grew serious. "And I do appreciate who he is. He's certainly entitled to some personal happiness, if he can get it, in his final years."

The doctor took another step toward him. "Jim, if you don't mind me pryin', what brought you down here all alone?"

"I was just taking some time out to think. To think and survey my record."

"Well, it's quite a record. One of the most impressive in the fleet." McCoy spoke with quiet earnestness. "And you did everything you could against the Klingons, and to save the children in this last crazy—"

Kirk laughed and shook his head. "Oh no. Not *that* record. No, Bones, I'm talking about conquests. And betrayals. Love enough to last a lifetime. That's given a week to prove itself. Soft night music. Drowned out by a computer's hum."

"The life of a sailor, Jim."

"Yes, it is." Kirk raised his glass, as if in a toast. "A girl in every port. And a heartache for every girl. Water, water everywhere . . ."

"And *you've* had too much to drink," McCoy said sharply, and took the glass away from him. After a moment, he drained it of its contents, and said thoughtfully, "Not bad stuff, this."

"Not bad at all, is it? Scotty gave it to me. After I convinced him I wasn't in the mood for Scotch."

They stood in silence for a moment, in the darkness, under the observation deck's great dome. Finally, McCoy said, "Jim, sometimes we all get . . ."

"I know, Bones, I know. And it doesn't mean anything. I wouldn't trade my life, this life, this ship for . . ." He looked around. "Just look at this ship that we're aboard, Bones. And look, look at the stars."

Again the officers of the *Enterprise* assembled in the transporter room, this time to bid farewell to Flint. He had refused Kirk's offer of a banquet in his honor and said only that he was anxious to return to his work.

"If I am to understand the communication from your Starfleet Command," he said to Kirk, "it appears the Klingons have not, through Kreth's experiences, learned enough to penetrate my cloaking device."

"No. Although seeing our use of fluorescence must have given them a clue."

"Ah, yes," Flint said. "Therefore, I hope to modify the Flint device so that it will screen out and disguise particles that collect around it, such as fluorescent dust. This will, hopefully, make it impenetrable once again."

Kirk smiled. "Unless you, sir, are called in again to crack it."

Flint's glance acknowledged the compliment. "It is a bizarre game, trying to confound oneself." He turned to McCoy. "Doctor. Has there been any further word on whether the Children's Center will permit me to take Pal as my legal ward?"

McCoy looked itchy and uncomfortable as he stood at attention in his dress uniform. "It's under discussion, sir," he replied. "Pal is receptive to the idea. It seems to have become a symbol of status among the

Onlies, the idea of having a 'Grup' of one's own. The main concern of the Center, though, is that Pal might be better off with other children about."

"Yes," Flint said, and paused. Then he said, "The planet of the Onlies is large, and, but for the Center, is now unoccupied. Is this not the case?"

McCoy looked uncertain, but Spock nodded. "Most of the planet was rendered uninhabitable by the genocide unleashed by the people of that world, in their madness, centuries ago. Devastation by fire, primitive bombs, and nuclear and chemical weapons. But, in areas like the site of the Center and hundreds of miles around it, all harmful elements have been broken down or washed away. Moss and woodland have taken them over. On other continents—"

"That's enough, Spock," McCoy cut in. "Mr. Flint didn't ask for a blow-by-blow geographical report on the planet's environment."

"This habitable land near the Center, Mr. Spock," Flint said. "Is it for sale?"

"That is unknown to me," Spock replied.

"Well," said Flint, "perhaps Pal will be able to gain a legal guardian and still have access to the Children's Center and his old friends. I've always been partial to moss-covered landscapes."

Of course, you can buy and sell anything you want to, Kirk thought, *love, family, planets, a man of your prestige can* . . . He winced, and told himself that now, at last, he would put away his unreasonable hatred of Flint and see him as a man with the joys and the tragedies, the strengths and the weaknesses of any man. Except on a colossal scale.

Flint stepped onto the transporter platform, where M-7 already hung, over one of the back pads, waiting patiently. "I thank you, Captain, gentlemen, for your hospitality."

"We thank you, of course, for all you've done," Kirk said stiffly. As Flint settled on a transporter pad, Kirk gave the order, "Energize!" and Flint and his robot companion dissolved and faded from view.

"It would be a good thing if he was to move to a place less isolated," McCoy remarked. "He's developing a few physical problems. Arthritis, a slight liver condition—nothing too serious. But in a few years, it won't really be safe for him on that planet all by himself. I as much as told him so."

"Indeed," Spock said. "Mr. Flint is a galactic resource of the highest order."

Searching his feelings, Kirk knew that he still had not forgiven Flint for his nameless crimes. He was glad that he would no longer have to force himself to treat well this man whom every foolish instinct told him to despise.

Spock gave him news which intruded on his thoughts. "Starfleet reports, Captain, that Boaco Six has expressed new interest in good relations. The admiral wishes us to proceed there now at top speed, and resume our diplomatic mission."

Kirk walked to a console by the door and flicked the switch. "Mr. Chekov, plot a course back toward Boaco Six."

Chapter Twenty-four

Captain's Log, Stardate 6119.2:

The emergency is passed. Although two of the children were lost, despite our best efforts, a galactic war seems to have been averted. We have heard no more claims from the Klingons that the *Sparrow* inflicted massive damage on their people or equipment. Apparently, Kreth's debacle has embarrassed them out of belligerency. The Federation has tried to estimate a fair sum to pay in restitution; the Klingons have accepted it without comment.

The Council of Youngers of Boaco Six now completely accepts the Federation's version of what happened when their ship and the ship from the eighth planet were destroyed. The *Enterprise* has returned to Boaco Six, in an attempt to capitalize on the restored trust and court the revolutionaries out of the Klingon-Romulan camp. We are discussing with them the possibility of better relations and aid, instead, from the Federation of Planets. Outlook: hopeful.

THE TOWERING, elaborately carved doors of the chamber of the Council of Youngers were swung wide open. Kirk led the entourage of senior officers from the *Enterprise* into the brightly lit chamber. The long table was covered with a cloth of wine-colored linen, and the glistening black brandy shimmered in precious metal goblets. Dress uniform was beginning to feel like daily garb for Kirk; he straightened up and walked forward to meet his hosts.

The entire Council of Youngers of Boaco Six was assembled before him. They were a forthright group of young men and women, some seemingly barely of their teens. The one older member of the council seemed incongruously gray and venerable. And there were four middle-aged men, who Kirk did not know, sitting at the end of the table.

The young soldiers had decked their chambers and themselves out with care. Tamara Angel stepped around the table and extended her hand to Kirk. Her garb was of the traditional woven cloth. She wore a gown of dark blue, with a stone brooch at her throat. A shawl floated around her shoulders. It was embroidered with spirals and tears and inlaid mirror-work. Her hair showered over it in waves.

"Captain Kirk," she said as she took his hand, "we are only too glad that you have returned to Boaco Six. We hope that we and the Federation can put behind us the misunderstanding that caused so much trouble when we last met. We are now more anxious than ever to increase good relations with the Federation of Planets."

"It is an honor and a pleasure to return, Tamara Angel. The Federation also feels that, now more than ever, we can only profit from closer ties to your world."

Tamara Angel led Kirk and his men to the table, where they formally greeted all the members of the council. And she indicated the four middle-aged men who sat at the far end. "And these gentlemen," she said with quiet pride, "are delegates who represent our neighboring planet, Boaco Eight. So, as you can see, Captain, negotiations are going on within our solar system. War between our worlds has been averted for the moment—perhaps forever."

The men bowed to Kirk and he bowed back. The *Enterprise* men were seated. Iogan was present, seated on Tamara Angel's right. Kirk was on her left. He watched, amused, as Iogan made a great show of pouring the goblets of Boacan brandy for the new guests, and as trays of food were brought in with great pomp and ceremony.

They may be revolutionaries, but they're learning quickly the need for social amenities, and the ways to fete and flatter us like diplomats.

Before the meal began, Iogan rose to make a toast. "To our friends in the Federation. May we learn not to falsely judge one another. And to respect our differences and recognize our common causes."

There was a general "Hear, hear," and the drinks were tossed off. Kirk remembered Tamara Angel's playful toast, "Here is mud going in your eye," and suppressed a chuckle. No doubt these kids would prefer to conduct negotiations in a relaxed and casual atmosphere, as he would. But the conventions would have to be observed. As exciting as power was, drudgery and the bourgeois art of compromise came with the territory; he was glad to see that they were learning that.

Now guards entered the chamber, carrying long wooden torches. They used these to light smaller torches which lined the walls of the high-ceilinged room, so that the light danced and crackled, and the room was filled with a mossy burning smell. The smoke drifted upward, through a vent in the distant roof. Mayori, the one old member of the Council of Youngers, shut his eyes and began to wail and chant in the ancient language of the people of Boaco Six.

"This is an old custom, Captain," Spock whispered, sotto voce, "at holiday feasts and great state occasions. They are honoring, with this torchlight, the two suns of their solar system."

Kirk could see that the men in the delegation from Boaco Eight were moved by the ceremony as well; they sat with their eyes closed and listened to the wailing.

When Mayori finished, more brandy was poured, and the young councilmen, acting as hosts, began the carving and the serving of food. There was a magnificent haunch of one of the six-legged jungle animals at the table's center, the skin sizzling and braised with a sweet-smelling sauce. The platter was garnished with herbs and wildflowers. There were delicately pickled small fish and fowl in small bowls, and skewers of chunks of some other kind of meat, wrapped in strips of seaweed. And there was a plate of spiced seaweed and a bowl of fruit for Spock. Kirk could hear McCoy baiting him, and Spock patiently answering as the doctor argued that Spock owed it to his hosts to try a little of the meat.

Kirk turned his attention to Tamara Angel, who was filling his goblet with brandy.

"Drink up, Jim. And whichever of us drinks the other one underneath the table shall be declared the winner at diplomacy."

"That's not fair, Tamara. You've grown up drinking this stuff. You'd beat me, hands down."

"Hands . . . down?"

"Never mind. It's good to see you again. I'm glad to

see you no longer think I'm a spy, or a fall guy for the Federation."

Tamara Angel looked apologetic. "We in the council wish to make amends for our earlier suspicions of you. And I must add my personal apology. We judged you too quickly and trusted your enemies too easily."

Kirk glanced past her to Iogan, who seemed to be debating some point across the table with the genial Noro. Kirk said in a half-whisper, "Then I take it Iogan didn't exactly bring back a glowing report of Kreth, and the Klingon arms dealers?"

Tamara Angel shook her head vigorously and also spoke softly. "He was disgusted by how they ran their ship, how they treated a colony they visited, how they treated him . . . and by their stupid destruction of the small ship you were trying to save. We do not believe in the senseless slaughter of small children, Iogan does not now think the Klingons are to be trusted."

"They're not exactly known for their winning personal charm. But I'm glad he was on hand for that graphic display of just how cruel and destructive they can be."

"Yes," she said. "And while we now know that the attack on Irina and the ship from Boaco Eight was, as you claimed, an accident, perpetrated by children who did not know what they were doing, other acts of sabotage we suspected Starfleet of have now been linked to the Klingons. We have evidence that they and the Orions are trying to force a war between us and Boaco Eight. They've been feeding us false information. Sabotaging our cargo ships and making it look like our neighbors are responsible, or the Federation. The Orions have apparently been trying to sell weapons to both sides, arm us both for the conflict.

We look upon war as a last resort—they try to push us toward it."

"Mmmm. Typical Klingon and Orion tactics. I'm glad to hear that you've come to recognize them." Kirk speared a piece of meat with his fork and sampled it; the meat was surprisingly sweet and tender, almost melted in his mouth.

Tamara Angel had launched into her food with gusto, seasoning the meat of the main dish with condiments, and biting chunks off the long sharp double-pronged skewers.

"But I take it then," Kirk continued, casually, "that the Romulans still have your trust? They are—besides us—the one power in the galaxy you feel you can do business with?"

Tamara Angel made a face. "I will tell you about the Romulans. I will tell you, now, of our recent close relations with them, because they are no more. Soon after you left Boaco Six, we commissioned a large supply of ocean transport vehicles, air-skimmers, and space weaponry from the Romulans. The most we'd ever spent on such a venture. The goods arrived several days ago. We paid in advance. Some of the flying machinery is acceptable and usable. But the weapons are outmoded junk. Not just primitive— they are old, burned-out weapons, unsafe to use. We have been ripped up."

"Off," Kirk corrected.

"Off," she agreed emphatically. "So perhaps you can see, Jim, some of the reasons why we are so eager to make a new start with your Federation."

"I appreciate your frankness, Tamara."

"I am authorized by the council to tell you, Jim, that we would like to begin trade again. Of the chemical argea, and our brandy, and other goods. But we must insist on fair prices. It cannot be as it was in the past."

"Yes, of course," Kirk said earnestly. He had some information that *he* had been authorized to convey, and this seemed like the time to pull out the Federation's most attractive proposals. "The Federation can give your people aid, Tamara, help you build argea processing plants here, on your own world. You could refine it yourselves, use it to benefit your people, and sell what you did not need to other companies in the galaxy at your own price."

Tamara looked cautious. "We are already too much in debt to the Federation. As it is, we cannot pay back the debts incurred by Puil and the other old tyrants."

Kirk had been waiting for this. He now offered his diplomatic plum. "There is talk in the Federation Council of canceling some of those debts. Erasing them. After all, Puil's excesses were hardly your fault. And we would like to see your world become self-sufficient, not more dependent."

"Erase . . . the old debts?"

Kirk was amused by her obvious surprise. "Fair treatment startles you, Tamara?"

"From the Federation . . . I'm afraid that maybe it still does. But you know, I think I could get used to it."

She smiled. The blue dress transformed the soldier completely into a vivacious young woman. Her maroon eyes twinkled.

"And as a further sign of our good faith, Jim, let me tell you some more news. 'Off the record' of course. I believe you will not be hearing any more about a Klingon-Romulan alliance. Iogan witnessed the beginnings of the discord. The Romulans wanted very badly to get hold of the Flint device, to penetrate it, neutralize it. They blame the Klingons for ruining the chance to do that. The Klingons are now angry that the Romulans sold us shoddy goods, and are making much of it, telling us that the Romulans are not reliable."

Kirk grinned. "I knew that it was a marriage that was too strange to last."

From across the table, Noro laughed and ventured a joke. "What is all this talk of a marriage that I hear? Have relations between us improved so rapidly?"

His joke was greeted with laughter from around the table, especially from the other members of the Council of Youngers. Tamara Angel rolled her eyes. "Honestly, Jim. Wherever we go to discuss politics, people form the wrong idea."

Kirk gazed back at her mischievous face and had to remind himself that this was a foreign minister of great importance, and the mission he was on was both delicate and grave.

Tamara Angel concluded what she had been saying. "So, while there are some on the council who still favor doing business with the Klingons and Orion, or with the Romulans, the general feeling seems to be that we want to give the Federation another chance. True, they have exploited us in the past—"

"Or, at least, some of its members have."

"All right, some *members* of the Federation, if you wish. At any rate, we are also aware that the Federation has done some good for the people of Boaco Six before our revolution, and set up aid programs like the one you now propose, although the corruption of the tyrants kept them from doing much good. But I think the Federation of Planets is the power preferred by the people of Boaco Six, as well as by the Council of Youngers."

"If you throw your lot in with us," Kirk said seriously, "I believe you will find that the Federation's attitude toward your world and your revolution has changed. We are more aware of the challenges you face . . ."

At this point, a slightly drunk delegate from Boaco Eight rose to his feet and made a long and tearful toast. A volley of toasts followed, each group present chiming in. The state dinner was considered a resounding success by all sides.

Chapter Twenty-five

ENSIGN MICHAELS had been on report since his outburst on the bridge the day of the battle with the Klingons. The captain had not summoned him to reprimand him; Michaels felt sure that Kirk was too furious to do so. In his mind, his misconduct superseded all other issues that Kirk might be dealing with, and he dreaded the confrontation that he felt must come, that he felt the captain was preparing for. He could not know that, when Kirk did find time to consider the boy's situation, he pondered how to advise him, in what direction to steer him, to help save his career.

In the days that followed the banquet given by the council of Boaco Six, Kirk gave the authorization for some ship personnel to beam down for shore leave; Michaels's name was ironically fifth on the roster. Kirk told Uhura to have him beam down; he'd talk to the boy at some point on the planet.

Michaels was relieved to be planetside again. He located his friend, the gang leader, who accepted him with some joking, and he brought presents for the boy's family. He could forget himself somewhat, forget that he was "in disgrace," and he wished that he could stay on this world forever.

He met a strange girl as he wandered through the streets of Boa. A rich girl from the Martian colony where he had grown up. Long blond hair, the best-tailored clothes—he knew a dozen like her. She came up to him at a festival dance, mocked his uniform, and scolded him for being at a Boacan holiday celebration.

"The people still know the truth," she said accusingly. "That the Federation is sabotaging this solar system. The people know it, even if the Council of Youngers has sold out."

She seemed to see herself as some kind of rebel. But her shrill, naive polemicizing caused Michaels to inwardly wince, as if at a cruel reflection of himself. He did not answer, just walked away as she stood there, shouting. He had never felt younger.

Kirk felt that the structure of these days on Boaco Six was a comfortable one in which to work; they were divided between formal negotiations and the relaxed enjoyment of Boacan hospitality. The city of Boa's noise and color, food, music, and brandy, curious animals, and friendly people calmed Kirk. Though he would, in sudden moments, get an itch to be back aboard his starship. Nevertheless, a vacation from the pressure did him good, and McCoy noted with satisfaction that the worries of Flint and the Onlies seemed to be drifting away from the captain. McCoy himself became engrossed once again in the jungle medicine being pioneered on this world.

But starships are not meant to be embassies, their personnel are not expendable for unlimited research.

Policy decisions would have to be made, civilians could better help reshape the muddled economy.

One ugly incident marred the pleasant atmosphere and drove this point home.

Kirk was accosted in the market by two men. One was tall and gaunt, with a piercing gaze. His head was covered with a dirty cap, and as he approached, Kirk saw soiled blond hair beneath it. So, then, not a Boacan. He was accompanied by a squat, plump Boacan boy.

He could not place them at first, then realized that they had disturbed him on his first visit. They had been following him.

"We must speak to you," the older man hissed.

"State your business, then." Kirk stared at him, hard.

"We are the alternative to this government. The alternative the Federation now wants to do away with."

"I don't understand."

"With Federation support we can defeat the rebel council."

"What support? Arms?"

"We can get argea to you. We can come to some arrangement—"

"Who are you?" Kirk cut him off.

The blond man took a step back, and the squat boy came forward. "My gang is small. But we are one of many. The city of Boa is honeycombed with such gangs, and if the Federation made it worthwhile I could convince many to join us."

"The Federation," Kirk told him slowly, emphasizing every word, "has no interest in your offer. We are negotiating with the planet's leaders."

The boy shrugged. "We already have support. Planets, groups within the Federation give us backing, have bolstered us for years. So, finish what you start."

"I have started a peace initiative. I intend to follow through."

The blond man again asserted himself. "We are not going away. You have not heard the last of us."

Kirk regarded him coolly. "Perhaps not. But the peace talks go on, regardless."

A loud noise from a neighboring street, that could have been metal cracking, or could have been a shot, caused the two men to start, then run for the cover of an alley. Kirk watched them flee, watched the dust settle in their wake.

The presence of Starfleet forces on Boaco Six was a temptation to such people. Kirk made arrangements with the Federation and the Council of Youngers for civilians to come in and take over.

He discussed the final arrangements with council members as they walked along the shore of the ocean, outside the city. For Kirk and his men, it was the last day on the planet. They had ridden to the shore on the backs of the bony, camellike larpas. The beasts seemed glad to reach the ocean, and now were stepping their hooves through it delicately, thirstily guzzling the cool black water with their long hairy muzzles, hooting happily to themselves. Apparently, the salt in the water did not deter them or harm them.

Refreshments for the Boacans and the men of Starfleet were served picnic style on embroidered blankets laid out on the sand. Several musicians sat on a rock and filled the air with their light, fluttering music. The sunlight shone off their instruments of metal and wood. Small, weird crustaceanlike creatures rose up out of the sand dunes and skittered past Kirk's feet into the water.

Kirk saw young Ensign Michaels kicking at purple pebbles and bits of driftwood that littered the beach, and walked over to him. He should have talked to Michaels sooner. He hoped the boy would be receptive to what he had to say.

"Captain," Michaels said now, "I wish to apologize for my behavior on the bridge. I panicked in a moment of crisis. I interrupted your thinking and planning at a crucial moment. In fact, my general behavior and performance of duty has been—"

"Belay that, Ensign," Kirk said gently. "And listen to what I have to say. I'm setting up a continuity team, to stay on the planet until the Federation diplomats and researchers arrive. Some Starfleet people should be here to advise them on how things stand, and to stay and work with them. Rizzuto, the historian, will be running this continuity team. He needs an assistant with enthusiasm, who has come to know and like the people here."

"I think, Captain," Michaels said carefully, "that I am not ready yet, perhaps, for the pressures of starship service. Maybe I could be more useful here."

Kirk gripped his shoulder approvingly. "Starfleet isn't the answer for everyone, Michaels. This job may grow on you. But while you're sorting things out and getting used to your work here, don't jump in with each new thought as soon as it comes to you. Just watch and listen . . ."

"And play it by ear." Michaels grinned. "I will, sir. Thank you, sir."

Kirk left him and headed on down the beach. The double sunlight warmed his back and his forearms through the cloth of his shirt. For the few days of their return to this world, he had been filled again with a sense of wonder at its dazzling beauty, color, and small creatures. He crouched and watched a group of tiny sand mites fighting over a large piece of salt. There was something about this world, the moist smell of the trees as the wind rustled through them, the feel of the air at night, the pulse of the local music . . .

What was it that the poet from the early Neptune colony had written when he first visited the aquatic world of Cestus Fourteen? "A planet drunk with springtime." And that was it, that described Boaco Six as well. A planet drunk with spring, drunk with life and growing. Drunk with sunlight—despite the dark cloud of terror and poverty that had hung over it for so long. He was struck, as he had been when visiting the Onlies at the Children's Center, by the resiliency of the young. Their stubborn, insistent, renewal and growth.

Kirk could see Spock engaged in earnest discussion with old Mayori, the council member who had led the torch chanting. They seemed to be discussing some point about the role of the continuity team.

Kirk had signed an initial nonaggression pact and trade treaty with the Council of Youngers. The Federation had given him the authority to do so, and Spock's logic had seconded what Kirk's instincts told him was the right move.

Kirk picked up a purple piece of coral, smooth as a sand dollar, and skipped it out across the dazzling black water. Waves crested near the shoreline and licked at the dry sand, then pulled back, bubbling with black foam. Farther down the shore, away from the clusters of people, Kirk could see Tamara Angel walking, wading in the shallows. She was dressed in her fatigues again, but her dark hair hung loose and shone in the glow of the suns. Her trousers were rolled up to the knees, and she stared at the water as she walked, looking serious and young. She paused, as he watched, and flipped bright orange seaweed up into the air with her toes. *No beach to walk on . . .* thought Kirk. Well, there were other compensations.

Tamara Angel became aware of him watching her, smiled, and splashed toward him. She explained, as she approached, that she hated wearing her boots on the beach. They slowly walked along together.

"So, in an hour you will be leaving us, Jim. I will be sorry to see you depart. It is a shame that we could meet only as actors for our causes, maneuvering, playing a complicated game."

They moved up from the water, and Tamara patted the bony flank of a larpa as they passed.

"I'm sorry, too, Tamara," Kirk said. "I hope I haven't in any way compromised your position, your situation as a government minister."

"Not at all, Jim. It is simply my misfortune to be a leader of people who like to tease. But perhaps you will come back to visit us someday? When we are less busy and relations are less tricky? Not as a special envoy . . ."

"I understand. I certainly hope I can come back. Your planet does me good. And I'd like to visit you."

"May you have many happy trails till then," Tamara said cheerfully. She caught sight of Iogan, who was glancing toward her frowning and beckoning. "Iogan worries too much. I think he is eager to have you leave. We have several formal events scheduled for today after this one."

"Like what?"

"This afternoon we are formally dedicating the Irina Memorial Peace Park in honor of our fallen comrade. The delegation from Boaco Eight will be there to say a few words about their diplomats who were killed that day. And this evening is the formal christening of Puil's palace, which you visited, as a national landmark."

Kirk recalled the palace, in all its grotesque opulence, the horrific torture devices and the mountain ranges of footwear and lingerie. "What are you going to christen it?"

"Well, the words are Boacan. Difficult to translate. I suppose the best English version of the name would be 'The Gluttony Monument.' What do you think?"

Kirk smiled. "I think it's a fine name, Tamara."

"I'm sure you would be welcome to attend both ceremonies, if you wish to stay longer."

The captain shook his head. "I would like to. But Starfleet orders dictate otherwise."

As they gazed out over the sand and across the expanse of the ocean, the sun-streaked maroon clouds seemed swollen with moisture and light. A cool breeze blew shoreward and tempered the languorous heat. Tamara Angel said good-bye and moved on to confer with Iogan. And Kirk began to gather his men to leave.

The crew on the bridge of the *Enterprise* was visibly pleased by their captain's return. Kirk asked Lieutenant Uhura to make sure that all ship's personnel who had been granted shore leave on Boaco Six were safely back on board. She confirmed that they were. Kirk paged McCoy down in sickbay, just to make sure the doctor hadn't lingered on the planet's surface to pursue last minute research. He invited McCoy to a game of billiards later, when they were both off duty.

Kirk checked in with Rizzuto and Michaels, and the continuity team that was remaining behind. They reported that all was quiet; they were going along to the peace park dedication. Soon Spock entered the bridge.

"I believe we have made admirable strides, Captain," he said. "The treaty you signed was a watershed. Even the venerable Mayori, long a foe of Federation aid, is coming to see the logic of it."

Lieutenant Uhura, who was busy decoding a news bulletin from Starfleet, now printed it out on a lighted tablet and handed it to Spock. He scanned its contents.

The turbolift doors opened and McCoy strode out. "Well, Jim. It seems as though your Vulcan first officer has lost himself a bet," he said.

"A bet, Bones?"

"His contention was that I'd hold up our beaming back on board, and get too swallowed up in the forest hospital I was visiting," McCoy said indignantly.

Kirk did not tell him that he himself had had a similar worry.

"But here I am," the doctor continued, "punctual and precise in the great Starfleet tradition! I made it back on board before he did."

"There was no actual wager involved, Doctor," Spock said, not bothering to glance up from the screen of the tablet he was holding, "but I am glad my ploy to increase your efficiency was successful."

"Efficiency, nothing. Seems to me you could help me out by reorganizing my little chemistry laboratory. I'll expect you down there at 1600 hours, and then I'll call us square . . ."

"I regret to say that the gratification of knowing that your work habits are improving must be your only

253

reward, Doctor," Spock said. "I would not presume to attempt to unscramble the arrangement of your chem lab."

Work on the bridge had stopped temporarily, as the crew listened to the exchange. Kirk suppressed a smile. He was beginning to feel very much at home.

"Hmph. Some sport you are, Spock," McCoy said. "I never trust a man who doesn't get into the spirit of gambling." He turned to face the captain. "Are you as sorry to leave that place behind as I am, Jim?"

"Yes, Bones. It's quite a rare and lovely little world."

Spock finally looked up from the news bulletin. "Much of this is irrelevant to our mission and our concerns, Captain. But not all. Some of the information here does concern Boaco Six and the threat of galactic war. Tamara Angel's analysis of the Klingon-Romulan rift, as you described it, seems to have been correct. The danger is past. Neither empire is willing to take on the Federation alone at this time. Or to make an issue of the Boacan system."

Kirk stared ahead at the black and maroon and orange planet his ship still orbited. Its image filled the screen. "Splendid, Mr. Spock. That limits conflict only to the craziness and discord within the system itself."

"The ministers from Boaco Eight who I talked to expressed to me great willingness to accommodate their neighbors, Captain, and share Federation support with the sixth planet. The threat of a war with larger powers intervening frightened them. Sanity seems to be prevailing on all sides." Spock, too, stared ahead at the bold little planet wrapped in the clouds, whose image bathed the bridge in a wine-colored glow. "We now have an unparalleled opportunity to

254

enhance the Federation's position in the area. If we use it properly."

"Let's hope we do, Mr. Spock. Let's hope we do." Kirk sat back in his chair. "Mr. Sulu, plot a course for the next quadrant and our rendezvous with the two starships there. Take us out of orbit, Mr. Chekov."

Once they broke orbit, the swirling world of Boaco Six and its three moons grew smaller and quickly vanished from the main screen. The twin suns of the Boaco system grew steadily smaller and fainter. But other stars beckoned.

Coming soon from Titan Books

DREADNOUGHT

Star Empire is the Federation's most powerful new weapon — a dreadnought, first in a class of super-starships — capable of outgunning a dozen Klingon cruisers, or subduing a galaxy.

On the eve of her maiden voyage, Star Empire is stolen by terrorists who demand a rendezvous with the Enterprise — and with Lieutenant Piper, stationed aboard Kirk's ship on her first training cruise. Now Piper must discover why her friends from Starfleet are among the terrorists… and why they insist the ship was stolen not to attack the Federation — but to save it!